Bargain On The Prairie

Rhonda Eichman

DWB PUBLISHING
www.dancingwithbearpublishing.com

~ One ~

A Whispered Prayer

Kansas Territory 1859

Annette DeSelvaine stood stiff against the blue and gray skies of the prairie. The early fall wind howled across the newly dug grave while she struggled with the full-length cape threatening to lift her into flight. Gripping the plush black velvet, she pulled the cape close around her small frame. The warmth gave no consolation.

Georgia Smith donated a blanket to wrap around the body of the thin, handsome Frenchman, before depositing him in the new territory's sod. Annette, numb to any burial preparations, stood mute through Georgia's orders, thankful the older woman took charge. A small group of farmers retreated to the side of the barn for a low-toned conversation, while Annette watched the bare earth at her feet in solitude.

Tony, how could you leave me like this, amid a bunch of ignorant dirt farmers? Annette turned to look at the ominous north sky that quickly began to swirl into a mass of gray clouds. She held her rage in check on a ragged breath. *They don't even have trees enough out here for a decent coffin!*

The air turned bitter and came about full force, hitting her in the face. Annette braced but the wind set her slight frame, seat first, on the sod.

Bewildered for a moment, tears streamed down her face too fast for the wind to dry them away. *Oh, Tony, I'm sorry. This is not your fault.*

Tony's uncle, Vicente Dubois, promised them a working share in his cattle ranch and real estate holdings when he learned of his only heir's wedding plans. Vicente begged them to wait until they reached his home in Southern California to wed and promised Annette a large wedding with all the trappings for a wedding gift. Her shoulders sagged against the weight of disappointment.

Annette contemplated the view, and decided dry dirt looked as hopeless as her future. Her mother's words rang in her ears. "Annette DeSelvaine, don't you dare leave this house with a penniless gambler. Your future is here, running my Palace, not out there in the west gallivanting around with that Frenchman."

The argument her father was a Frenchman only served to heighten the madam's growing rage with her daughter. "If you leave my house with him," Mrs. DeSelvaine paused to give the ultimatum significance, "you'll not be welcome here ever again."

Annette did not say a word. She hung her head in disappointment, sulked to her room and changed into one of the servant's gray work dresses to escape the house, taking only a dark, velvet cloak to ward off the night chill. She ran to Tony's rented room, and by dawn, they were on the road to a new life. Annette knew she could not go back, and now her only hope of escape was buried six feet underground.

What good is a wagon full of flour and beans and four spirited horses? Annette wiped the thought from her mind with a violent shake of her head. She knew she would rather die than go back and fulfill someone else's dream of what life should be. She did not want the life her mother did. Annette sat on the ground rocking back and forth. "My God, what am I to do?" Her voice became a mere whisper with the wind careening across the flat plains of buffalo grass.

~ * ~

Cole Waldren leaned against the tightly stacked sod that made up Tom Smith's shabby excuse for a barn. Cole's crop of blonde hair resembled the haystack he lost to a twister last summer. His oversized hands tried to smooth the mess of straw into something presentable, while his stare never left the young woman by the grave. *Why doesn't she stand up or does she intend to sit there all day?* Cole watched her rock back and forth and knew she cried for the man she lost.

A prickle ran down the back of his neck and he felt Ellie Wilks staring at him again. Her sharp brown eyes could burn a hole right through a man. He self-consciously squared his stance toward Annette and stuffed his hands into his pockets.

Cole turned and peered at Ellie distastefully, trying to repress a visible shudder as he thought of the only eligible woman in this part of the territory. Her waist-length blonde hair fully made up for her lack of delicate features, and she displayed ample curves. Cole could hear his father's voice.

"Marry Ellie and set up housekeeping. The

9

meadow north of here is open for homesteading, and it would be a fine place to start." He took only part of his father's advice and staked a homestead claim on the acreage to the north, which included the meadow. In self-defense, Cole directed his concentration back to the gathering.

~ * ~

"Don't appear she's used to fending for herself out here in them fancy slippers and velvet cape," Ellie said jealously. Her hands unconsciously pressed the rumpled calico skirt over the generous curve of her hips. "I say we send her on in her expensive wagon with those worthless racing horses." Her eyes lingered on the delicate features of the pale face at the graveside. "What fool would hitch a team of racing horses for hauling?" She turned up her nose at the dead man's folly.

"Ellie." Reverend Schmidt looked sternly at the young woman. "There will be no turning out any of God's creatures to certain death when I be about. Winter will be here in a few weeks and she would be dead first snowfall. We have to offer her shelter until the next wagon train comes through, or until we take the herds to the pens near Mud Creek come spring."

"Who's gonna put her up? We barely got food enough to see ourselves through the winter," John Wilks said. Ellie's father stared bleakly at the beauty seated on the sod and wondered how his own daughter would take this newly arrived competition. He knew his daughter acted like her mother, bullheaded and sharp-tongued. John rarely thought of his dead wife, and he could see the same woman in front of

10

him in the person of his only daughter.

~ * ~

Cole attempted to walk in the direction of the grave. His shoulders strained forward but his long legs refused to move. The girl remained seated on the ground, and although she stared in his direction, the blank look on her face told him she saw nothing. Ellie cast a smile in Cole's direction and the frozen legs instantly unlocked. Cole made long strides across the prairie toward Annette and stood before her. Annette looked up—way up.

Annette calculated the young man stood well over six feet and had beautiful blue eyes. His face and hands were deeply tanned, and his shoulders and legs heavily muscled. The winds blew his loose shirt in around him, and she could see his stomach all but caved in. His hands were calloused, and he needed a haircut but stood confidently in front of her, seeming completely at ease.

"I'd like a word with ya, ma'am." Cole began with a slight hesitation and extended his hand. She accepted the offer and Cole pulled her to her feet, but she kept distance between them.

Annette busied herself brushing away small broken stems of buffalo grass from her cape, avoiding his intense gaze.

"I think you're in kind of a fix out here in the middle of nowhere with losing your man and all." Cole cleared his throat and stumbled onward. "What I'm saying is, you can't get back East or wherever until spring, and there ain't nobody else here could put you up for the winter. You sure can't live in a wagon with weather like we get in the winter."

He paused for a breath. "I be needing a woman around the house for cooking, chores and housekeeping. I'm the only one with cabin space and supplies enough to board you through the winter, but I won't move you in unless we're married." He spoke plainly and glanced around to avoid looking directly at her. "I figure we could make a right good bargain, both being in need and all. So, we might as well get married up before the preacher leaves. He won't be back till spring neither, so you see, your only chance for shelter is now or never."

Annette stopped dusting herself mid stroke. She looked at Cole and tried desperately to close her gaping mouth. When it finally snapped shut, she bit her lip to keep it closed. *The nerve of these miserable dirt farmers.* Annette looked again at the wagon and horses, angry they brought her here, then at Cole in disbelief.

Cole saw her studying the rig and horses and jumped to his own conclusions. "You give me the rig and horses for a dowry and we have a bargain." Cole gazed out across the grassland, looking anywhere but at the girl, wondering if she would ever speak.

"How close is the nearest town?"

Cole frowned. "That would be the abandoned site of old Fort Atkinson, about hundred or so miles through Indian country. The trip would be a week or so ride for a good rider and rifle shot like the preacher." Cole pointed at Reverend Schmidt. "Unless Satanta and his braves show up."

"Can I get a coach back East from there?"

"No. There's nothing back east until spring and the last wagon train came through during the

12

summer months. I already told you." He sounded an-
noyed at having to repeat his words.

"I'll go with Reverend Schmidt to the fort. I'll
get a room and wait there until spring." Annette felt
new confidence surge through her while she devised
her plan and ignored Cole's outrageous offer.

"There are no rooms to rent at Fort Atkinson.
The army abandoned the fort several years ago, and
soldiers use the place occasionally to rest between
excursions to the western edge of the territory. Only
cavalry soldiers stop by the place." He paused. "Men
who haven't seen a woman in months." She stared,
eyes blank, and he could not decide what she might
be thinking. "There's no women there but I can't say
as you wouldn't be welcomed." Cole's eyes roved
openly over the petite curves even a full cape could
not hide. He detected the start in her eyes, so he
added, "with open arms."

"You mean I'm stranded?" Annette choked.

"Yep, woman. Ain't you got ears?"

Annette hung her head in disappointment,
contemplating her predicament. *A fort full of men
with no female companionship? The fort would not
be much different from her mother's brothel.*

~ * ~

The Palace sat at the end of a street lined
with Spanish moss-covered trees creating a canopied
private lane in a wealthy downtown area of New Orleans. The rock structure, surrounded by a black iron
fence, served as a combination gambling hall on the
main floor and a brothel on the second level. The
third level luxury flat served as living quarter for Annette and her mother.

13

Annette became an expert at dodging her mother's customers, and the slaves always helped. She remembered Magnolia's strong black hands tenderly stuffing her into a large laundry basket and piling sheets on top of her.

"What you be needin' in here, Misser Simmons?" Magnolia asked the man who pursued Annette into the kitchen. Magnolia continued to chop innocently at a leg of lamb with a large meat cleaver, then stepped back and held the cleaver in mid-air, waiting for an answer. "They's ain't nothing in here you want. What you want is out there." She pointed to a stairway leading up to a large sitting room on the second level.

"I, uh, I lost my way..." Mr. Simmons stuttered, and backed out of Magnolia's kitchen.

~ * ~

There would be no Magnolia at Fort Atkinson. Annette's only other choice for survival stood in front of her. This tall, rugged man appeared to be in the habit of telling others what to do. Her anger rose in tears and dropped silently on her black slippers making shiny dots on the dusty toes.

Cole, growing impatient, dropped to one knee to try and get an answer. When he knelt, he could look her in the eye, since now they were the same height. Cole cupped his hand under her chin and raised the small face for a better look. The large, dark eyes were wet and miserable as a sick colt, and he could not remember ever touching anything as soft as her skin. Cole at once hated himself for his lack of compassion for her grief. He thought how

14

frightened and alone she must feel, and he remembered the feeling in his heart when he buried his
folks.

"I'm no good at words, especially soothing
hurt feelings. I know what grief feels like when
somebody you love dies. Everything inside kinda
curls up and don't wanna uncurl. After a while the
pain won't be as bad. I'm not saying the hurt ever
goes away, but things get better after some time
passes. I'm really sorry you lost your husband, but—"

"Tony was not my husband, and I would appreciate if you would address me by my name, which
is Annette, not woman."

Cole's jaw dropped. He tried to snap his
mouth shut. "You mean you're a tainted wom—" Annette's raised hand warned him to stop or wear a
red mark across his face for the rest of the day.

She set the line of her jaw straight and looked
directly into Cole's eyes. They were handsome eyes
set in a strong face. Not a handsome face, but a rugged one with strength. Eyes tell all and Annette
thought she should not have blurted out the confes-
sion, yet, she did not want to lie. "I'll accept your
offer, if you're a man of your word and don't go
back on bargains," she said firmly.

Cole caught his breath and his insides quiv-
ered. He wondered at the emotions welling up inside
of him, anger mixed with joy. Even when she needed
help, this woman would not accept orders and did
not hesitate to call him on his words. *She's got guts.*
"I made my offer, and I'll hold to every word."
Cole's face flushed red-hot and he struggled to get
his knee straight. He extended his hand and Annette

15

took the offer. Together, they walked toward Tom's barn and a new life in the new territory.

Bargain On The Prairie

~Two~
The Wedding

Ellie watched the couple at the graveside, who appeared to be talking. *What could Cole be doing down on one knee?* She looked back at the group and no one else seemed to notice. They were all intent on finding a solution for the problem of the pretty stranger in their midst. She turned back and thought she saw the young woman raise her hand to Cole's face. *What could he have said so out of line*? She certainly would not have considered anything Cole said out of line no matter what he might suggest, and she found herself day-dreaming of Cole's arms around her. She dropped the fantasy and watched the couple walk toward the group.

Annette and Cole went to Reverend Schmidt. "Can you marry us up before you go back?" Cole asked.

The reverend looked startled but not as started as Ellie, who stood behind him. Ellie's expression did not escape Annette's sharp eyes and the hatred directed at her.

"Do you willingly agree?" Reverend Schmidt looked at Annette.

Annette looked at him and said firmly, "Yes, I agree to this marriage and I want the ceremony today, please."

"Then today is the day for a wedding. Everyone, come gather in front of the barn and let's get this wedding started." Reverend Schmidt's excited voice called the group together.

"The food will have to wait," Georgia started giving orders. "Everyone find chairs and benches for the men to line up in front of the barn."

"We need an altar of some kind," Jennie said.

"Will my washstand do?" Georgia asked and raced into the house to get the stand and find the Bible she saved since Susan Waldren's death. She recalled the promise to give the Bible to one of her boys' brides when the time came. Both of Cole's brothers left to stake their own claims after their parent's deaths, and only Cole remained on the homestead. Georgia thought Cole would never marry after rejecting Ellie's advances. She rummaged through the large, old buffet against the wall and found the worn, black leather volume.

The other women left their food preparations and hurried over to Annette, prying her from Cole's arm.

Georgia led her inside and beamed with enthusiasm when she gave Annette the Bible to carry down the aisle. "This Bible belonged to Cole's mother," she announced placing great importance on the statement.

"Thank you," Annette said and set the Bible on the bed as the ladies helped her out of the heavy cape. They all agreed the gray dress to be simply too plain.

"I do have something packed away. I'll be right back." Georgia said and left the room returning with a long, pale pink satin gown. The sheath style dress had darts under the bust and a simple rounded neckline. The dress displayed tiny pearl buttons down the back, and the sleeves were long and edged in lace. The slim skirt did not have a bustle as current fashion trends dictated.

"When did you get this?" Jenny asked, stroking the fine fabric.

"I made the gown for something never meant to happen," Georgia said sadly, and all the women were quiet for a long moment.

Annette stood in front of the long mirror in Georgia's bedroom and looked at the girl in the reflection. Her dark hair hung to her waist in long curls against the pink satin. Her face, still pale white, reflected a hint of the gown's pink color. Her brown eyes gleamed with teardrops waiting to spill over.

The pink sheath fit against her laced-up bodice, hugged her flat stomach, and followed the curve of her hips to spill on the floor. She reached down to gently lift the excess satin in front of the gown, so she would not trip over the hem. She made her way out of the bedroom slowly and cautiously, which made her movements appear graceful and serene.

"The gown is absolutely perfect for you," Georgia said. "Please keep the dress as a remembrance of today and the start of your new life." She buttoned one last tiny button on the edge of the long sleeve.

Annette choked out, "Thank you."

Jenny handed her the Bible topped with a fall bouquet of dark red and yellow marigolds. Even though the flowers did not match, they contrasted perfectly with the pink gown.

Annette followed the women outside and walked toward the barn. The women lined up and finished their encouraging comments to her, then went to sit with the men. Annette looked at Cole standing with the preacher.

Cole's eyes locked on hers and his mouth gapped open. He starred for a long moment, and finally managed to close his mouth and swallow.

"Annette, would you please come forward?" Reverend Schmidt asked, and she walked slowly across the carpet of buffalo grass to Cole's side.

Reverend Schmidt read the words directly from the Bible and Cole said his 'I do's' in a shaky voice. Reverend Schmidt never saw Cole frightened before this moment, not even when they hunted down a mountain lion last year, but he could see fear in Cole's eyes now. Reverend Schmidt amused, smiled to himself. *Cole is in for a change and Annette looks to be God's answer for what Cole needs.* He tried to get Cole to marry Ellie, but this new woman would do fine.

Annette's 'I do's' on the other hand, were firm and confident, she even smiled at her new husband. Reverend Schmidt wondered about her past predicament since she so willingly moved into a new situation, although, he really did not see an alternative for her at this point.

After the quick ceremony, Reverend Schmidt said, "May I introduce Mister and Missus Cole Waldren."

Applause erupted from the group, except for Ellie, who stood with both arms crossed. She frowned at the couple when Cole escorted Annette to the barn where the rest of the women set food on the tables. He found a clean bench by a small table and spread his jacket so Annette's gown would not snag on the rough wood.

Ellie looked in distaste while he fawned over his new bride.

Reverend Schmidt noted the change in Cole's behavior already. *Nothing like a lady to make a man act like a gentleman.* He smiled, well satisfied with his latest task of joining couples.

"Cole, will you lead us in the mealtime prayer?" Georgia asked.

"Come Lord Jesus be our Guest and let these gifts to us be blessed, Amen." Cole smiled at An-nette.

Annette listened intently to the words her new husband said. She watched everyone bow their heads and repeated the behavior because she didn't know what else to do. Magnolia prayed many times, always with her hands raised to heaven and her eyes wide open, looking up like she saw the Jesus to whom she prayed.

Annette found comfort knowing he appeared to be a Christian man, unlike Tony, who acted po-litely when in the company of others but never treated her well when they were alone. She knew from the beginning Tony, selfish at heart, saw to his own needs first and hers second, if at all.

She suddenly remembered Magnolia telling her, "You don't need to be with no gambler like Tony, Miss Annette. You need a good man who loves the Lord." Magnolia knew everything about her since

21

childhood and Annette did not keep the secret of Tony from her lifelong nanny. Annette found a small sense of safety in connecting those words with Cole.

"Would you like to accept the congratulations from the group with me?" Cole asked.

"Yes, I'd like to meet everyone," Annette replied. The new couple accepted congratulations from the group. The women embraced Annette warmly, the men clasped Annette's hands with theirs and were as welcoming as the women. Then they turned to Cole and shook his hand.

Only John Wilks gave her a shrug with his hands shoved deep in his pockets. His daughter, Ellie did not come through the receiving line. Instead, she went to the table, loaded a plate, and stuffed food in her mouth, picking the best from the table.

Annette looked at her and wondered where she received her training in manners. Ellie's long blonde hair showed sun-bleached streaks. Tall and full figured her thick fringe of glossy bangs, large lips and a small nose gave her a pouty look. She knew Ellie's look from the girls at the Palace most of the men preferred. *Ellie would have fit in perfectly.*

Cole escorted Annette to the buffet when the receiving line finished, and Annette took the empty plate handed to her. She selected what fresh vegetables there were, lean meat, and only one slice of dark bread. Annette noted Cole selected a couple of large biscuits, jam, meat piled high, and some potatoes. She mentally logged his preference for food when he led her to their small table and asked if she would like something to drink.

"Yes, coffee would be great, if not, water will do." He returned with two large mugs of hot coffee and slices of pie balanced on top of the cups.

"Would you like some dessert?"

"No, thank you."

Annette used her best manners and ate her food slowly. Despite the events of the day, she was famished. She hadn't eaten since early morning when she and Tony tried to travel west across the prairie.

Cole starred at her intently and she met his stare with equal concentration. They were both down to the bottom of their coffee. "You like coffee, too?"

"Oh yes, I'm afraid I developed the habit early. At least we have something in common."

The rest of the afternoon and evening gave Annette a good picture of the warm pioneer people with whom she now shared her life. They seemed genuinely glad she was now a part of their community and they were willing to help her make a fresh start in the territory. All except for the Wilks family, and Annette suspected she interrupted a matchmaking plot with Ellie and Cole.

Georgia rose and began packing away the leftover food for each of the families to take home. She suddenly remembered why the small community got together—a funeral. She set the dishes down and retrieved the small cross set out earlier and set out in the direction of the newly turned grave. Georgia placed the cross upright in the freshly turned sod. "Rest in peace, Frenchman."

She turned and saw Annette standing behind her. "Quite the day." She hugged Annette to reassure her. "The Lord brought you here for a purpose and He will take care of you. Place yourself in His hands."

Annette stood silently looking at the grave, remembering Magnolia always saying God would take care of her. She drew in a deep breath, but still the tears would not spill over.

Georgia began to guide her back in the direction of the barn. "I'll be by to check on you in a few days. Anything you need, let me know then. Make a list as you think of things and I will help you. This is a good place out here in the territory and you'll be safe with Cole looking out for you. Cole's a fine, God-fearing man. He will never allow any harm to come to you and will care for you like his own body."

Annette thought how strange the phrase sounded, 'care for you like his own body.' She did not know what the words meant but logged them in her memory until she could figure them out later.

Cole met them halfway and put his arm around Annette. "Thank you, Georgia for the fast organization of the day."

"She's mighty tired, time to take her home."

"I'm headed there," Cole assured her, and escorted Annette to a buckboard by the barn.

Annette leaned on Cole's arm. He picked her up and set her on the seat with ease. Annette sat close to him to ward off the cooler temperature of the fall evening. Cole finally reached behind the buckboard seat for her cloak and wrapped her in the velvet. She gratefully acknowledged his care with a smile but remained quiet, deep in thought while the team of horses followed the dirt road home. They rode under full moonlight to Cole's place in silence. Two hours passed, and Annette realized they saw no other cabins. The vastness of the empty prairie only added to her feeling of emptiness.

~ * ~

Ellie sat beside her father on the buckboard with arms crossed and a defiant look on her face. John knew his daughter wasn't happy with the competition the afternoon delivered. *She's fit to be tied.* He knew she shamelessly threw herself at Cole only a couple of weeks ago after Sunday services.

Cole had leaned against the back wall of the barn when Ellie approached him, and he watched her press her body against Cole and then reached up to stroke his hair. Cole, completely taken by surprise, pried her loose and gave her a shove. She looked as if she might topple over, but then caught her balance avoiding a fall. She placed her hands defiantly on her hips and gave Cole a good tongue-lashing. John could not hear Cole's reply, but Ellie's face turned bright red and she ran to the house.

"What are you thinking about?" Ellie asked, angry at the world.

"Oh, that little episode behind the barn a couple of weeks ago with you and Cole." John looked at her. "Ain't no way for a young lady to act."

"He shouldn't have pushed me."

25

"Looked to me like he needed to push you," John raised his voice. "I'd better not ever see you conduct yourself again in that manner." He whipped the horses into a faster trot.

You certainly won't see me. I'll look around first to make sure you are not spying on me the next time I find a man I want. Ellie kept her arms crossed defiantly and moved to the far end of the buckboard seat.

~ * ~

Cole pulled up to the small ranch house with his new bride, and his horse tied to the back of the buckboard rig he borrowed from the Smiths when he was asked to help with the Frenchman's body. He planned to take the rig back to the Smith place to-morrow and bring back Annette's covered wagon. He looked at his home and thought how small and insig-nificant the wood and sod house looked in the full moonlight. The barn loomed many times larger and looked to be of better construction than the cabin. His mother always wanted a large log home, but his dad built the barn first. Sam Waldren never made good on his promise to build the log house.

Cole worked on the small cabin in the winter months when time allowed. He reinforced the loft and completed minor repairs. Both the front and back porches displayed new flooring. He built special screened doors to fit outside the larger outer doors.

A limestone cliff loomed over the meadow of bluestem grass behind the house. His herd of cattle grazed in the meadow and on the hillsides behind the house to the far north edge of his property. A narrow creek trickled past on the south edge. A stand of cottonwood trees struggled for life, taking hold by the stream and followed the line of the creek to the east edge of the property. The limestone cliff at the back edge of the meadow offered protection from sharp winter winds, and Cole thought the area would make a good place for the herd to winter.

He helped Annette from the buckboard and even thought her might carry her across the threshold as custom dictated, but she bolted out of his hands and onto the porch in one quick movement.

She opened the door and peered into the darkness. *There is no place to run and hide in this tiny cabin and no servants to protect me.*

"I'll light the lamp and show you around." Cole held the lamp high and the yellow light cast shadows on the large bed against the back wall of the room. The front part of the house held a sofa, a large table with four chairs, a wooden cupboard, and a countertop with a sink. A large dresser hugged the back corner and a wide plank ladder led up to the loft over the kitchen area. "There's another smaller bed in the loft you can use." Cole pointed to the ladder.

Cole saw fear in her eyes. Her hands trembled even though she clasped them tightly together.

"I'm no animal, Annette. I am not going to attack you. We've both been through a long, grueling day. You need some privacy and some rest. The bed in the loft is yours and you can wash up with the basin on the stand up there. There's also a chamber pot under the bed or you can take the lantern and go to the outhouse behind the cabin."

He paused and watched her shoulders relax with relief. "I'll go put up the rig and check my cattle. I'll be on the porch until the lamp goes out, then I'll come in. Good night." He turned and walked out.

Annette stood frozen for a minute. Anger replaced fear. *Does he ever stop ordering people around? Could he not think to ask what I would like or what I wanted or needed?* She grabbed the lamp in one hand and hitched up her skirt with the other. She knew she would fall if she attempted the climb without a free hand and began unbuttoning the dress.

There must have been a hundred pearl buttons that seemed to take forever to unbutton but finally, the last one came loose, and she wiggled out of the form fitting gown, letting the fabric fall to the floor. She grabbed the dress and threw it over her shoulder. With the lamp in one hand, she used the other to navigate the sturdy ladder with ease. When she reached the top, she set the lamp on the floor on one side of the ladder and deposited her gown on the other side. She crawled over the edge with significant effort and into her sanctuary.

She saw a comfortable single sized bed covered with a warm, handmade quilt. A small nightstand stood next to the bed, and a two-drawer dresser stood against the wall with a bowl and pitcher. She placed the lamp on the nightstand and sat on the bed, wonderfully soft but not made for sitting.

She suddenly felt relieved to have some privacy and peace, but also very tired. She would have to sleep in her under garments, but the corset had to go. She folded the pink dress neatly on the chair, then washed her face and hands and fell onto the small bunk. Remembering the lamp, she sat up and turned down the wick. She fell into deep sleep when her head hit the feather pillow.

Cole starred at the ladder, quiet for a long time. He watched through the window to make sure she could navigate it and decided to go in and help when she began unbuttoning the tiny pearl buttons of the gown. Helpless to look away, he starred when she wiggled out of the dress. Finally, he left the front porch to go to the barn but could not go any further than the edge of the cabin. He leaned against the solid wall and regained his senses.

After a few minutes, he went to unhitch the team. He led them to the barn and returned to sit in the rocker on the front porch until she extinguished the lamp.

He retreated to his bed and tried to find sleep that evaded him. Cole finally got up when he could see edges of the new morning beginning to show. He dressed quietly and left out the front door to return Tom's buckboard and get Annette's covered wagon and horses back to their new home.

~Three~

The Cache

When Cole reached the Smith farmstead, he put the buckboard wagon in the barn and the horses in their stalls. He walked toward Annette's covered wagon and saw the team still hitched to their harnesses. They were tired and needed water and rest. He jumped aboard and took them back slowly. When they arrived, he pulled the covered wagon to the backside of the barn and unhitched the horses. He rubbed them down and placed fresh hay and water in each of their stalls. He could see they needed better treatment than they received from Tony.

With the animals taken care of, Cole decided to climb into the wagon and have a look. Shocked by the amount of supplies stashed under the seats and in the grub box, Cole unloaded the wagon. A full winter's supply of beans, flour, sugar, baking soda, baking powder, coffee, lard, bacon, and a few potatoes filled the wagon. There were pots and pans and a nice iron skillet.

Cole found Annette's trunks of clothing and hauled them out first. *She'll want something clean when she wakes.* When he opened the first trunk, and saw most of the items untouched, still with store wrap on them. The second trunk held leather riding pants with matching jackets, a new cookbook, and an apron. He placed the trunks on the porch, pulled out a crisp green print dress with some fresh under things, and took them into the house, leaving the heavy trunks on the porch.

Cole entered the house quietly. There were no sounds coming from the loft, so he climbed the ladder and peered over the edge. She slept on her side, with her dark hair cascading across the bed behind her. Her thin arms stretched across the bed as if she reached for something, while one of her hands dangled over the edge of the bed. Her body, partially covered with the blanket, let one bare foot find a path out of the covers. He simply starred for a long time, then placed the folded items from the trunk on the floor near the ladder where she would find them when she woke. Cole backed down the ladder and thanked the Lord for the quiet sturdy frame constructed by his dad.

Cole went back out to the wagon and began taking supplies to the lean-to against the barn. He put the last item away and set the pots and pans out to take into the house. With no noise from inside the cabin, he decided to sweep out the wagon, take the canvas top down, and store it away in the barn. Earlier, when he lifted Annette's trunks out of the wagon, he saw an uneven plank on the wagon floor under the trunks. Cole bent down to examine the plank further. The wood slate appeared out of place and not nailed down, so he pried the wood up with a crow bar. He could not believe his eyes.

The long, narrow space was full of cash bundles, a leather bag, and a small derringer. He remembered seeing a gambler at Mud Creek use a derringer like this one. He fully examined the entire wagon for other hidden compartments and found

31

another with jewelry and more cash bundles that amounted to a small fortune. He could not imagine what the jewelry could be worth.

He placed all the items in a long, wooden box and took it to the loft in the barn. He hid the crate under the eaves his dad used for hiding valuables. He didn't think Annette knew about the cache and decided he would tell her later. For now, the items were not his and he decided not to touch them. His part of the bargain was for the rig and horses and did not include the money and jewelry. *If she knew about the items, would she take them and leave in the spring?* His thoughts abruptly ended when he heard her.

"Cole. Cole, where are you?" Annette stood on the front porch with her hair back in a topknot and hands planted firmly on her hips.

Cole came out of the barn. "Yes, ma'am, coming."

"Sorry, didn't mean to pull you away from your chores. I only want to know where the supplies are, and I need the pots. I'd like to make some coffee and fix breakfast, if you're hungry."

Cole grabbed the skillet, and an armful of pots and pans and stepped up his pace. He arrived on the porch in a second. "You can cook?"

"How does biscuits and gravy sound?" Annette smiled.

He helped by preparing the coffee and starting a fire in the large black stove while Annette put the biscuit dough together and fried some bacon. Cole could prepare coffee but knew nothing else about kitchen tasks. He stood helpless except to watch her well-practiced movements in the kitchen. She finally asked him to pour the coffee and set the table to get him out from under her feet in the small space.

Cole never tasted anything so delicate and light. He stuffed the first biscuit into his mouth whole. He prepared to devour the other biscuits lined up on his plate with gravy in an almost ceremonious act, evenly spreading the creamy white gravy across the golden-brown tops, then he precisely quartered and stabbed the first section. He hesitated, looking at the food, inhaling in the steaming fragrance.

Annette giggled. "Are you going to eat them or just keep arranging them?"

Cole stuffed the first quarter of a biscuit in his mouth and followed it with another quarter before chewing. The biscuits and gravy melted in his mouth.

He asked, "What else do you need to cook in your new kitchen?"

"Once I have a look at all the supplies, I'll know. Eggs would have tasted good with breakfast this morning. Do you have chickens?"

"No, but I can get us a few and there's meat, salt pork mostly and dried beef jerky. I think I might butcher a cow and rebuild the cold box for storage. Tom and Georgia have a large cold box."

"Do you mean an ice box?"

"No, a cold box. A hardwood box placed underground near the stream to keep meat cooled down. What's an ice box?"

"It's a large box with a solid block of ice in

33

the bottom. There was one in the kitchen at the Palace. Every other day someone came and brought a new block of ice."

Cole complemented her many times during the meal for her cooking skills. "I have a lot more questions about the Palace but have to tend to cattle and won't be back until nearly dark."

"Alright, I'll clean up the kitchen and check supplies for my list then go outside and look around."

"Watch where you walk outside. We have snakes here."

When Annette finished the kitchen chores, she examined the cabinets and noted everything needed cleaning but could wait for another day. Magnolia always said cleaning expands to the amount of time available, but always waits on you. Annette laughed with new understanding.

She found her trunks on the porch and decided they were too heavy to drag into the cabin, so she unloaded her clothing items an armful at a time and put them away in the loft. She found her aprons and hung them in the kitchen on a peg near the stove and placed her cookbook on top of another one she found on a shelf. Her first tasks finished, she ventured out to see the sun high in the afternoon sky.

September afternoons are beautiful here. She walked around the small house and the enormous barn. She found her wagon and the lean-to where Cole kept supplies. She could tell Cole took pride in his possessions and took care of what he owned. All

the tools hung neatly on hooks and the horses buried
their muzzles deep in their feedbags. Their water
buckets were already half empty, so she refilled
them. She found a bucket and the pump behind the
house and completed her chores.

Tony did not care for the horses and simply
used them up. They looked downright skinny. She
petted their noses, a habit she developed when Tony
bought them in Kansas City. She sat on a bale of hay
and took in the smell of the loose straw. *What a
comforting place.*

She put her feet up for a break from her work
when she saw them. The tiny kittens came around
the corner of the door and meowed for their mother.
A skinny old cat came out and starred at Annette.
Annette's presence didn't seem to bother her, and
she went to find a spot to lie down in the sun and
nurse the kittens. Annette watched but didn't try to
touch them.

When the kittens finished nursing, Annette
found a pan, and filled it with water. The mother
cat drank and rubbed against Annette's skirts, then
crouched low and prepared to rid the barn of one
more mouse. Annette watched and thought about
the cats at the Palace who got milk in a bowl and
scraps on a plate. They wouldn't have known what a
mouse looked like if one stood in front of them.

Annette ventured out to the back of the property where a large rock cliff backed up to a meadow
of soft grass. She heard the stream at once and
walked toward the sound when she saw something
move. She remembered Cole's instructions, stopped

suddenly, and waited. The brown and white snake raised a triangular shaped head, coiled up and began shaking its tail, which made a distinct rattling sound. Annette moved backward and decided to explore the meadow another day.

A bare patch of earth behind the house looked to have been a garden already harvested and put down for the winter. A much smaller plot than the one Magnolia kept in the back of the Palace looked to have been only an underground crop. Annette found a couple of small potatoes and one large on-ion.

She decided to check the lean-to and see what else she could find and found cured salt pork, lard, more potatoes and onions, oatmeal, flour, and sugar. *This will do nicely,* she smiled to herself and went to the kitchen.

Cole walked up on the porch and smelled salt pork frying with potatoes and onions, along with the scent of something he didn't recognize. He entered the cabin and found Annette using a spatula to slide small, flat cakes from a cooking sheet to a plate. Cole peered at the fragrant smelling cakes. "What are they?"

Annette looked at him in disbelief. "I found oatmeal in the lean-to and decided to bake some oatmeal cookies for dessert."

"Cookies? I haven't had a cookie in a long time."

"Your mother never baked cookies for you?"

"Only a couple of times." He hesitated, look-ing like an eight-year-old child. "Can I have one?"

"Sure, but only one, I've cooked for an army."

They enjoyed their evening meal and dessert with the late afternoon sun streaming through the kitchen window. They talked until the sun became moonlight.

When she mentioned the snake, she saw the blue color of his eyes change to a steel gray. Annette, oddly surprised, thought he might already be protective of her. Magnolia always protected her, looked out for her safety, and added what she could to her happiness.

"The snake is a prairie rattler and very poisonous. One bite and you can die if we don't get the poison out quickly. I'll go to the meadow tomorrow afternoon when they are out sunning themselves and do some shooting. If you ever suffer a bite, you must walk, not run, back to the house. Get the gun from the rack over the fireplace and fire a shot in the air, and I'll come."

"What will you do then?"

"I have to cut the bite and suck out the poison."

"I don't know how to shoot a gun."

"We'll have to tackle shooting too, first thing tomorrow."

She thought he looked tired and wondered if he slept at all last night. Time would not have allowed him to take the rig back, get her wagon, unload, tend to the horses, and sleep. She would wait until tomorrow to ask him to move her trunks into the cabin. She starred into his eyes and thought she made him blush.

"I need to go to bed. I am completely worn

37

out," Annette said.

"I know what you mean." Cole got up from the table to go out on the porch until she extinguished her lamp.

Annette lay in her bunk contemplating her first day in her new home. *He is kind and I enjoyed our hours together at the table tonight.* She would have to give this some time. She knew a long winter stretched before her and decided things would be fine until spring when she could ride to Mud Creek and get a stage back to Kansas City. She didn't have any idea where she would go from there. *There is nowhere else to go,* was the last thought to cross her mind when sleep overtook her.

~Four~
Daily Life

Georgia and Tom Smith began their morning early and decided to take their coffee on the porch. This would be some of the last few days for a morning warm enough to sit outside. Georgia found she already needed a shawl for her shoulders and scooted closer to Tom on the hard, wooden bench.

"I wonder how the newlyweds are doing?" Georgia asked.

Tom shrugged, remembering the previous morning when he saw Cole return the buckboard and left with Annette's covered wagon. *Much too early for a new groom to be up and about.* Tom judged Cole's actions silently and decided not to start any rumors about the couple.

"I wouldn't go running down there first thing."

"Oh, Tom, I wouldn't intrude. I'll wait a few days and then check in on them. Don't know if they even have anything to eat."

Tom gave up and knew Georgia would do exactly what she wanted.

~ * ~

The day began much like the first day of marriage for Cole and Annette with breakfast and a few chores. Annette noticed her empty trunks placed on the opposite side of the fireplace from another one. She decided to store some of the blankets and linens in the trunk after she washed them in the laundry

39

tubs she found in the barn.

Cole took his Sharp's lever action rifle from over the fireplace and asked her to come with him to the barn. On the backside of the barn were four bales of hay stacked up to chest height, and another four bales several yards out with an old paper tacked up on them.

"Need to teach you how to shoot so you can fire a warning shot if needed. I don't expect you to ever hunt or shoot anybody, but you need to be able to sound a warning. I'll take care of the hunting and anybody who gives us any trouble. Cover your ears until you get used to the sound." Cole brought the gun up to his shoulder and fired off a shot. Even with her ears covered, the sound made Annette jump.

"You don't really have to shoot at anything but if you don't and you miss, the shot will carry farther than you can see, so try to aim at something." He reloaded the rifle, handed her the gun and helped her fit the butt of the weapon against her shoulder. "Don't pull the trigger until I say to squeeze."

Cole came behind her and placed his arms around her, held up the gun, and pressed the rifle butt into her shoulder. "If you don't bring the butt all the way back, the rifle will kick you black and blue." He placed his hands on hers and guided them to the trigger. "You're going to aim at the paper on the bales and squeeze the trigger."

He could feel Annette shaking with fear. "Please don't be frightened. You need to know how to shoot, but you don't have to shoot every day." He pulled the rifle up to her shoulder again. "We're going to pull the trigger." He squeezed her hand and the gun went off.

The power of the shot pushed Annette backwards against Cole's chest. "I think the rifle is going to knock you down when the shot goes off. Let's try again and brace yourself with your legs spread apart." Cole reloaded, and they tried another shot. "Enough shooting for today until we see how your shoulder looks in the morning."

They walked back to the house and Cole unloaded the gun. "I keep the shells in a carved box on the mantle and the gun goes on the hooks over the fireplace. I'm going down to the meadow and see if I can find some snakes to practice on." He opened a trunk by the fireplace, strapped on a holster with a pistol, and tightened the belt low across his hips, tying the leather straps down on his right thigh.

"Can I come watch? I'll stay back out of the way. I really want to see this." Annette sounded intrigued.

Cole nodded. "Sure, you can come with me."

They stopped at the barn where Cole got a bucket and a baking soda can from the shelf and they walked out to the meadow. He found a spot by the stream where a fallen tree lay in the shade giving some seating and checked the area for snakes. "You can watch from here, but don't move around. I need to know your location at all times."

Annette watched him make his way across the meadow in a crisscross pattern. Occasionally, he stopped, squared his stance with legs spread apart, drew his gun and fired, then returned the gun to his holster. He walked with purpose and never shot twice. He stopped to reload the Sharp's four-shot pistol once, then took a long stick with a forked end and re-traced his footsteps. He scooped up a dead snake with the forked end and hung the snake on the lowest branch of a nearby tree. When the shooting ended, eight dead snakes hung in the branches. He pulled out his knife, cut off the rattles, and placed them in a baking soda can. He then cut off the heads and placed them in a bucket.

"Why do you cut off the heads and tails?" Annette asked as they walked back to the house.

"I cut off their heads, so I know exactly where the fangs are located. A dead snake can still kill if the fangs full of venom puncture you. I will bury the heads deep in the sod and I keep the rattles for trophies. I have several cans of them. The snake meat will feed something tonight, probably coyotes."

"What's a coyote?"

"They look like a dog, but they're not. They are a predator and they howl. We'll hear them tonight. See you later. I'm going out to check some cattle." Cole placed his pistol back in the chest near the fireplace.

Annette spent the rest of the day exploring the house and found some heavy iron muffin pans with six slots shaped like ears of corn. She decided to make corn muffins. She went to the lean-to in search of corn meal, potatoes, onions, and salt pork.

What a strange place. A comfortable cabin, and a dry, dangerous outdoor environment. There are no graveled streets or street lights, very few people, and only one other person to converse with for the entire day.

With plenty to do, she felt challenged by the tasks, and the man named Cole. Only a glimmer of regret for Tony invaded her thoughts. There was no deep grief for him and she felt a bit guilty.

Comfortable at once in the kitchen, she started the list Georgia knew she would need, truly grateful to have a friend. She missed Magnolia and longed to spend the day with her learning a new recipe. They spent countless hours at the Palace in the large kitchen where Magnolia cooked for up to thirty people at a time. Annette found herself cutting the recipes down to size in her head, which proved to be no small task. She moved a few items around in the kitchen to suit her cooking style and this evening, she produced a hardy meal of fried salt pork, potatoes and white gravy, and cooked carrots. She baked two loaves of fresh bread and pulled them from the oven.

"What's the heavenly smell coming from the oven?" Cole came in from the barn as soon as he smelled food cooking.

"White bread. Do you have butter?"
Cole went to the back porch and brought in a tin can sitting in a bucket of cold water. "Have some right here."

He set the lump on the table next to the bowl of mashed potatoes. Then he eyed the gravy with a sinister gleam in his eyes. "You won't last long," he said to the bowl and Annette laughed. Cole said grace the same way he did at their wedding and dug into his food.

43

"What did you eat before I came and started cooking?"

"Mostly jerky or sometimes I'd fry some salt pork or venison and potatoes. Never had bread though, this is good. Where did you learn to cook, from your ma?"

"No," Annette hesitated, "from my nanny, Magnolia."

Cole starred at her. "You mean like a servant or something?"

"Yes. Magnolia is a slave in my mother's house."

Cole stopped eating and glared at her. He wasn't sure he heard her correctly. "Your family owns slaves?"

"My mother owns several."

"What about your father?"

"My father was a gambler and left before I was born." She looked up, watched Cole's face to gauge his reaction, and did not like what she saw. Cole looked saddened by the thought and then angry.

"What about your parents? What did your mother cook here in this kitchen?" Annette asked attempting to change the subject. She didn't know how Cole would react to her story of growing up in a brothel, but she already could tell he did not like the fact her mother owned slaves.

Cole didn't answer until he finished the meal. Thinking of his mother's corn muffins and how they were like the one's Annette baked, he suddenly missed her, and longed to talk to her about Annette. Cole drew a deep breath and began his story.

"My folks came from Wisconsin and home-steaded this acreage. Dad wanted grassland to graze cattle, so we added two additional sections to the original ones. My mother did not like to cook and did very little, mostly meat and potatoes and, sometimes corn muffins. There were three of us boys and I am the oldest. The other two took off after the folks died.

You know there's probably going to be a war over this slave question. Do you own any slaves or only your mother?"

Annette did not like pointed questions. "Since I was a child in my mother's house, I did not own anything or anyone, Cole." She was firm with her answer and decided to get the remainder of the story out in the open. "Since my mother chose to be a madam and run a brothel, she did not have time to raise me. The job fell to her finest slave, Magnolia. I received my education in private schools back east and with tutors when I lived at home. During my time at home, my mother restricted me to either the kitchen with Magnolia or my room on the third floor. I still love Magnolia like my own mother."

She stopped for a deep breath to calm herself but felt anger rising within her. "I would never choose to own another human being and if I ever found myself inheriting slaves, I would free them at once." Annette's voice continued to rise in a crescendo with the final note at a full yell.

"I will not be told how to think or what I should believe. You do not own me. I have a mind of my own." When she realized how loudly she spoke, she simply stood and left the room.

45

Cole sat at the table for a long while. No one ever yelled at him. Finally, he got up and went out to the barn. He found Annette sitting on a bale of hay petting one of the kittens. He picked up the kitten and sat down beside her.

"I didn't mean to upset you. You don't have to think the same way I do. You've got a right to think differently. I know we're from two different worlds and I got a lot yet to understand. I know I don't own you or your mind." He sat in silence for a full minute with the kitten on his lap waiting for Annette to speak.

When she remained silent, he said, "None of us can change anything about our parents or how they lived or believed. We can only get out there on our own and be what we want to be and try to figure out how we think things should be. I'm sorry, I didn't mean to upset you. And I won't try to tell you how you should think." Cole began to pet the kitten but promptly put the tiny animal on the straw floor of the barn.

"Why did you stop petting the kitten and put her down?"

"I've never petted kittens before and I'm not sure what I'm doing."

Annette looked at him and burst out into laughter. "Never had enough cookies as a kid, never petted kittens, good heavens. What have I gotten into?" She clasped her face in fake dismay. They both laughed in relief.

"I promise I can learn both." He picked up the kitten and petted the tiny animal who returned a ferocious purr. "Are we too late in the day to bake cookies?" They walked to the cabin arm in arm.

~ * ~

Annette pushed back the loose strands of shiny black hair. Sweat poured off her forehead. Her arms hurt, and her palms began to blister. Amazed at the intensity of the heat during the midday hours, the territory weather surprised her at how quickly the air cooled into the evening hours. When she awoke, she found Cole turning soil with a shovel in the early dawn hours. The turns produced a few more potatoes and onions for the lean-to.

"You might want to rake the ground smooth. I'll lay straw on the top for the winter and we can keep harvesting a small crop of potatoes and onions from under the straw. You'll find tools in the barn."

Can't be too difficult, she thought until she raked the soil for an hour. With blood running down the rake handle, she knew she must stop. Annette retreated to the house and poured cold water over her raw palms.

Cole came in the front door. "The meadow to the south of the house will be good grazing area for the cattle." He stopped mid-sentence when he saw the red water in the basin. He came to her side quickly and lifted one hand from the water. His eyes widened with concern when he saw the open sores.

"Let me get some ointment and bandages for the wounds. If your hands get infected, you are going to be in real trouble. We've got no doctors and no sulfur."

Cole returned after scrubbing his hands with harsh homemade soap. He began gently blotting the wounds with clean rags. After the bleeding subsided, he applied the ointment and clean bandages. "Don't want you out there anymore. The dirt can cause infection in the wound and this must stay completely clean. I can finish raking the garden this evening and you can watch from the rocker on the porch."

Where did the tyrant go who ordered her to work this morning? A strange mix of emotions surged inside of her, anger one minute, grateful the next. As soon as Cole left the cabin, Annette, completely exhausted, collapsed on the end of her bed falling asleep at once.

She woke mid-afternoon, realizing she missed lunch. She climbed down the ladder and winced when she gripped the rails, suddenly remembering the blisters. She found the loaf of bread on the table and cut a thick chunk and added a generous helping of butter and berry jam. After polishing off a slice, she cleared away the crumbs and looked at the clock. Time to think about what she would prepare for supper.

She noticed Cole washed the dishes and left her a note instructing her to not put her hands in dirty dishwater until the wounds healed. He must have come back to the cabin while she napped, and she didn't know why she felt guilty that he washed the dishes. Her mother never allowed her to work or do chores at the Palace. The only exception was cooking with Magnolia. She felt determined to learn her new routine and not be a burden to anyone.

~ * ~

The late October days shortened and grew colder and Cole came home earlier each day. They had been married for a month and had grown comfortable with their routine. They also read the Bible together some evenings and discussed what each thought of the verses. Annette learned easily and began to understand the full light of her mother's sins, and of her own. She saw how selfish she truly was and determined to think of others first.

Annette was quiet, not participating in the reading with her usual comments. Cole knew she was deep in thought about something and said, "Let's pick up here tomorrow evening. We both need some sleep."

~ * ~

Cole fell into a fitful sleep, tossing and turning. He worried about getting Annette, himself, and his cattle through the winter. Cole dreamed about the money, the jewelry, and the derringer in the barn. He dreamed he saw Tony pointing the derringer at someone and awoke, frightened for Annette.

He tiptoed to the loft to make sure she slept peacefully and watched her for a few minutes before he backed down the ladder. He decided there must be much more to Tony than Annette knew, and he thanked God she ended her journey with him near his homestead.

She is everything I ever wanted.

He knew sleep had ended for the night, so he decided to leave early to bring the cattle down. from the plateau north of the cabin and winter the herd in the meadow where he cleared rattlesnakes earlier in the fall. Then he would move some feed there and hoped they lived through the rough winter.

Annette awoke to an empty cabin. She drank her coffee alone and thought of Tony and how he had spent every evening on the journey in a saloon or gambling hall. He claimed to be an expert gambler and bragged he earned their way with a turn of the cards. She knew he also carried a derringer in his coat pocket for protection.

She wondered what he would do with his evenings when they left the eastern part of the territory and the towns disappeared. She found out right away. He simply drank liquor and lay by the fire.

One evening in Kansas City, Tony came back to the wagon at a dead run, completely out of breath with his jacket pockets bulging. When she asked what happened, he simply said some men were sore losers in a poker game and he had to outrun them.

Annette knew when Tony lied but she could not pry the truth out of him. A few weeks later, they reached the western side of the Kansas territory and he came down with a cough and fever. She knew from seeing the illness before at the Palace in New Orleans, Tony suffered from consumption. Three of the girls at the Palace died after contracting the illness while Annette ran a fever for less than eight hours with a light cough. Magnolia took care of her and Annette didn't even know if her mother realized she had fallen ill.

~Five~
Hunting

The days blurred into one another. Annette lost track of what day of the week it was, until she found a calendar in an almanac next to Cole's bed. She intended to mark off the days since the wedding but found Cole circled their wedding day and marked off days in the same manner she used to do back home.

She loved sitting on his big bed. The mattress felt firmer than hers and she laundered his sheets regularly. Laundry proved to be the hardest of all the chores. The washboard and large basin in the barn were adequate but shaving soap into shreds proved to be too much of a chore.

"Could you shred the soap for me, and bring a couple of buckets of hot water from the house to the barn? It's really getting too cold to take a bath out here without warm water."

After one of her baths, Cole appeared at the barn door wanting to check for any more black and blue marks from the weekly shooting lessons. Securely wrapped in a large bath towel, he examined her shoulder and back. "We need to suspend the shooting lessons, you still show blue and green discoloration. Maybe we'll get you a derringer in the spring, something you can handle."

She found herself wondering what happened to Tony's small pearl handled derringer he always carried in the inside pocket of his coat. She thought the small gun might still be with Tony's body in the pocket of his jacket. However, her thoughts stopped when Cole's large hands touched her shoulder. He left the barn and she dressed quickly and wrapped herself in the velvet cloak and ran to the cabin.

"I know I'm full of requests this evening, but could you also bring in one of the tubs from the barn? I found some lengths of fabric in a trunk where you keep your pistol and decided to make some long curtains to draw over an empty corner near the fireplace. I think one of the metal tubs might fit behind the curtains for a private bathing area."

"I'll get the task done before freezing weather comes across the plains," he promised.

~ * ~

Annette found some bushes near the meadow and knew at once what kind of berries they produced. She picked every berry and baked some into a pie and cooked down the rest for jam. Several pints stood on the window sill cooling in the evening air. Annette traded some of their pantry items to Georgia for other items she needed.

Cole judged the supplies were still plentiful for the winter months. He bought a few chickens from a neighbor and they were taking over the barn, but they did have eggs. They would need a chicken coup by springtime, but he would need to pick up lumber for the project when the group went to Mud Creek in the spring.

Georgia came by weekly and Annette looked forward to her visits. "Georgia tells me there are some wild turkeys sometimes near the grove of trees down the roadway. Do you think they are still around? We only have a couple of days before Thanksgiving."

"I think I might be able to find us one. You want to go with me?"

"I'd love to. I've not ventured very far either direction on the road and I'd like to know more about this place I'm calling home."

Cole took the scattergun down from the rack and asked, "Can you ride a horse, or do you want me to get the buckboard out of the barn?"

"Oh, I can ride." She only mentioned to Cole once about riding but didn't elaborate on the fact she enjoyed riding lessons at boarding school and competed in jump competitions on the East coast. During riding lessons, she gave up the ladylike sidesaddle and rode astride wearing riding pants. She went to her trunk and retrieved a pair of the soft leather pants Tony bought for her in Kansas City. She retreated behind the bath curtain to change and then meet Cole in the barn.

"Can I ride the brown one? She is smaller and more my size."

Cole turned to answer and pushed back his hat for a better look at his new riding partner. "Well, I'll be. Pants? No sidesaddle? Those look right nice." He looked her up and down. "So, you can ride," he said.

He cupped his hands to hold her foot, so she could mount the horse. Annette accepted the step up to the saddle and rode out of the barn door before Cole. She drew up in front of the cabin, breathing in the fall air, and grinning.

Cole guided his horse up the dirt road and motioned for her to follow. They road at a gallop until they neared the grove of trees then slowed their pace. "We'll dismount and tether the horses, so we can walk up. Don't want to scare off the turkeys if they're in there." Cole dismounted and helped Annette with her dismount. He drew his scattergun and they walked to the grove.

The trees stood naked, most of their leaves gone and provided very little cover. They could see completely through the stand of growth and they saw no birds. He thought Annette looked disappointed.

"Let's sit behind the sand plum bushes and the turkeys may come in around early evening." He motioned to four large sand plum thickets. They crept in behind them and sat on the ground.

"These bushes produced tart red plums at the end of summer. Pheasant, quail, and turkeys like to come in and clean up the fallen plums. They might make some pretty good jelly. I'll have to pick you some when they come in next year."

"I can come down and get them since I know where they are," Annette beamed.

"I need to go with you when you pick. I killed a mountain lion in here last fall. Guess he liked the game coming in too. He took a calf of mine and I tracked him for weeks into this thicket. These thickets are full of thorns and I'll be glad to pick for you," he motioned to some of the needles still showing.

Annette turned to look at the opposite side of the grove and Cole followed her gaze. He whispered,

54

"You've got good ears, little lady. I didn't hear them. Lay down on your stomach so they don't see us," he stretched out.

Annette looked amazed at the line of large round bodies sitting atop long skinny legs. She would have to ask later why turkeys walked single file. Then the flock spread out suddenly and began to graze, pecking at the ground.

They lay close together and Annette wondered why Cole took so long to line up his shot. She knew he did not need the extra time and she turned her head to gaze into his eyes. He wasn't watching the birds at all. He was enjoying the scent of her hair.

"Ok, I'll shoot."

She covered her ears in response and he took his shot. Annette squealed in delight and ran to the fallen bird scattering the flock.

Cole followed her drawing out his knife and grinning. "Hunting's fun," but he did not remembered hunting with his brothers being this much fun. "Let's field dress the bird and we'll finish back in the barn."

~ * ~

When Georgia pulled the buckboard up to her home, she saw Ellie riding in and wondered what mischief the girl could be up to this morning. Ellie waved to her and Georgia asked, "Won't you come in and have some tea this morning?"

Ellie agreed, and they sat at the table visiting about the small community's news events. Ellie knew when the snows started, travel would not be possible, and she wanted to catch up on local gossip and events.

"Where were you coming from in the buck-board when I rode in?" She asked Georgia.

"Gone to see the newlyweds."

Ellie wanted to know all about the new cou-ple, but Georgia seemed guarded with her comments not wanting her to know Annette still slept in the loft. Annette did not say anything, but Georgia saw Annette's items on the loft floor and knew she slept there.

"Annette can cook and Cole's ribs aren't showing anymore, and she can sew too. The cabin is clean and there are new curtains hanging."

After a few minutes of listening to Georgia sing Annette's praises, Ellie thanked her host for the tea and rode home. Georgia waved goodbye from the porch.

After putting a half mile's distance between her and the Smith homestead, Ellie doubled back through the wooded area behind both properties and came up behind the Waldren property. She tied her horse to a stump and followed the creek to the back of the Waldren barn. She could see two of the horses were still missing and she entered the cabin through the back door.

She searched everywhere. She opened Cole's wardrobe but saw only his clothing and none of An-nette's. She crept to the front of the cabin and climbed the ladder to the small loft where she found Annette's clothing and items stowed away, along with a pitcher of fresh water and towels on the washstand. Ellie knew then Annette slept in the loft, not downstairs with Cole.

56

I still have a chance. If they aren't sleeping together yet, then something must be wrong. Maybe the little dark-haired girl doesn't want Cole and truly only needs a place to winter until she can leave in the spring.

This new discovery lifted Ellie's spirits and kept her hopes alive. Her thoughts drifted back to the summer picnic in the meadow with Bobby. New to the settlement, everyone felt optimistic Bobby would claim land and start a homestead. Others in the settlement sent back east for their relatives, they stayed, and the community grew stronger with each new family. However, summer's end saw him leave without a word of goodbye.

Ellie saw the loaf of bread on the kitchen table and her stomach growled. She grabbed the loaf, stuffed the prize under her jacket and slipped out the back door.

The cabin had been lonely since John left more than four weeks ago, and he had never been gone so long before. With all the food in the cabin gone, she would have to forage for roots in the woods or trap a rabbit but in the meantime, the bread would be good.

~ * ~

Annette and Cole pulled the horses up to the barn and tied them to the railing and went inside to take care of the turkey Cole shot. Annette, intent on watching the process, marveled at his knife skills. The bird, plucked of its feathers and rinsed, was placed in cold salt water to soak overnight. Cole added southern whiskey and honey to the brine before he covered the metal tub with a second, heav-

57

ier tub to keep any intruders out for the night.

Annette helped Cole with feed and water for the horses, tagging along to be near him. They left the barn together, walking arm and arm to the cabin.

The only food available for the evening meal was left over fried chicken and potato salad, and Cole agreed the small cold meal would be great. Neither of them seemed very hungry this evening.

"Can we ride together more often in the afternoons?" Annette asked.

"Of course. I'm excited you can handle a horse so well," Cole said.

He asked her about the jumping competitions she took part in back east in Virginia and was amazed at the breadth of her skills. He thought she would be good at whatever she chose to tackle.

"Will you put the turkey into that large baking pan and load it into the oven?" Annette asked.

"Of course, I'll be happy to help you."

The coffee perked on the stove and filled the room with a rich aroma that mixed with the scent of turkey cooking in the oven.

Annette sat at the table with a small cookbook open to pages marked, "A Thanksgiving to Remember." The only item lacking for the dressing were celery stalks and they simply did not have any. Next year she would make sure she saved back some from the garden, and then she caught herself. That would happen only if she stayed.

She had traded Georgia a loaf of bread for a

pumpkin. Turkey, dressing, mashed potatoes, and gravy were on the menu, along with hot yeast rolls, butter, corn cut off the cob and pumpkin pie.

Cole came in from the barn like clockwork when she pulled the pan of biscuits from the warmer. He poured their coffee and they sat down to start their day.

"Annette, this looks good!"

The morning conversation centered on their plans for the day. Cole assured her, "I'll be back by noon and spend the rest of the day with you and we'll go for a ride."

Annette found herself smiling when she tackled the cooking chores. The yeast rolls were rising and potatoes boiling when she sat down at the table to pinch the edges of the pie crusts. Annette completed this routine many times in the kitchen with Magnolia and felt grateful for the years of instruction.

Cole came in after only a couple of hours and wanted to help with the cooking. He completed a few of the heavy tasks, pulling baked items out and getting the heavy pots and pans out when she needed them. He helped with dishes after the meals now, and never let her work alone. She sent him to fetch a tablecloth from her trunk, and he brought in some fuzzy, brown cat tails from the creek to place in an empty vase. He set the vase in the middle of the table with some dried, long blue grass stems.

"How perfect," she said, surprised by this side of him.

They sat down and said prayers of thanksgiving for the food. "And for this wonderful woman placed in my path," Cole added.

They finished the day together with a long ride until nearly dark.

~Six~
The Big Cats

Annette awakened to complete silence. Daylight filtered in through the windows but there were no sounds of Cole making coffee. She peered over the railing expecting to see him stepping into his jeans and pulling on his shirt. The cabin felt empty, and she sprang down the ladder to find a note on the table. "Gone to bring the cattle down from the hills, weather's coming in. I'll be back at dark, Cole."

She noticed the loaf of bread and berry jam missing from the table and the beef jerky bag out and felt guilty he left without a good breakfast. She started the coffee and contemplated what she would do for the day.

She decided to clean out Cole's area at the back of the large room. So far, she laundered his sheets weekly and decided to go through the dresser and the tall cabinet, scrubbing all shelves and adding fresh packets of herbs she made. Fragrant herbs and seeds covered the prairie floor and she gathered the bounty on her walks. Using her reference book, Annette drew sketches of each one in a small notebook and filled small sachet bags and the whole cabin smelled clean.

After a quick cup of coffee, she tore into the area. Scrubbing and creating piles of items to launder or mend. She found books and old almanacs with references to cattle numbers, sale prices, and the cost of supplies. She was careful to replace them in their exact order knowing they were valuable references for Cole.

Cole only owned a few shirts and she found one in shreds. She decided to use the shirt for a pattern and set the ragged piece aside. She would decide which of her dresses to give up for fabric later and she would make him some new work shirts. She found his boots, cleaned them, and washed the dresser top.

There were references in his current almanac about the number of cattle he owned and a reference about her. He scribbled and underlined *She can cook*. Annette smiled to herself when she read his comment and put the almanac back exactly where she found it.

Cole walked in the back door at supper time. He spent many hours of the day tending to the cattle in the meadow behind the cabin. After the evening meal, Annette cleared the table and the two fell into their routine of conversation and reading.

"Do you want to study the Bible with me in the evenings instead of only reading?" Cole asked.

"Yes, I like to study."

He produced a study guide Reverend Schmidt gave him years ago.

"Were the words Reverend Schmidt read at our wedding from the Bible?"

"Yes." Cole got his Bible from the dresser and turned to the pages Reverend Schmidt read at their wedding. Annette moved from her chair across the table to sit next to him to see the words. They took turns reading.

"So, your job is to protect me and care for me like your own body, to even give up all things for me?"

"I think you are correct. I will protect and care for you. I need to do the demanding work, so you don't hurt your hands. Can I see them?" He took her hands and looked at the healing blisters left by the rake. "I'm so sorry. I should have never asked you to rake the garden. I didn't know you would get blisters."

"You could not have known. I always worked in Magnolia's garden, but only planting and pulling weeds. I never handled the shovel or the rake. I will speak up if you ask me to do something I have not done before. Maybe we can get some gloves for me whenever we go for supplies."

"We'll get you some in the spring to use for picking berries or gathering herbs, but you will not be raking the garden again." He sat quietly starring at her, secretly wondering if she would stay in Mud Creek with him come spring.

Cole said a silent prayer asking for God's help but could no longer concentrate on reading. "Let's finish reading tomorrow night and we'll find out what you're supposed to do. It's getting late." He went to the porch to allow Annette her privacy.

Cole thought about the pure joy he felt and could not help but smile. Happier than he could re-member, he knew the profound loneliness of his daily life for the last two years had disappeared. He loved coming back to the cabin and sharing his day with Annette. "I think I might be falling in love," he said to the cat, who sat on the porch with him.

~ * ~

Annette felt refreshed while preparing breakfast. Both had slept in a little longer since sunrise came a little later in the morning. Cole did not have to go far to check the cattle in the meadow near the back of the property, and she could hear them through the open kitchen window.

Cole finished his oatmeal and went to the barn to move some feed to the new bins he constructed at the corral. The hay and feed he bought last spring still took up space in the barn. Cole decided to run a pipe from the well to a stock tank and set up a float on top of the water, so the windmill would pump when the float declined in depth and stop when the water level reached the top of the tank.

Annette looked in wonder at the construction. "When did you do this? I'm amazed I didn't hear you working."

"Did most of this project last winter and stored the pieces in the barn. I cut the corral lengths and slotted the railings, so they would go up without nailing. The round stock tank, leaning against the outside wall of the barn, only needed to roll downhill. I set up the pipe while you were busy sewing on something at the table. What were you working on?"

"New shirts for you. The ones in your dresser are getting pretty shabby and kind of tight," she said and touched his chest where the shirt he wore pulled hard at the buttons. Then Annette ran her hands across his chest to get an idea of the width she needed for the shirts.

"I need to get your measurements, so I know where to set the seams down the sides. I can measure you this evening after supper."

Cole's breath caught in his chest, and for a moment, he couldn't move. He spent the rest of the morning moving the heavy shocks of feed to the bin at the corral and wondered at the anticipation he felt at the thought of Annette measuring him.

~ * ~

When Cole came back to the house for lunch, he saw Annette on the porch with kittens in her lap, and the mama cat sat at her feet content to let Annette handle the kittens. There seemed to be a lot Annette could handle with ease and some things she could not.

He thought about her hands, which were healing nicely, and the black and blue on her shoulder was fading. Even though he knew the shooting lessons should continue, he decided he did not want her hurt or bruised and vowed to buy her a small derringer in the spring. He noted Annette peered down the roadway like she saw something.

"What you are looking at?"

"Not sure, I thought I saw something moving, maybe a dog?"

Mama cat jumped to her feet and Cole thought he startled her, but the cat looked down the road also. He looked for a long time, and then he saw the animal.

The muscles across Cole's stomach tightened. "No, too fast and too big for a dog or a coyote. Let's get in the house."

Annette set the kittens on the chair and Cole

held the door for her. Mama cat began picking up her kittens and running them into the barn one at a time and Annette became alarmed. Cole closed the heavy wooden door behind them and went straight to the fireplace. He opened the chest, took out his Colt pistol, buckled the holster low across his hips, and tied the leather strap tight against his right thigh.

"What is out there?"

Cole loaded the gun and returned the weapon to his holster, then took down the long gun and loaded it. "I think we've got a cat come down for the winter."

"What kind of cat?" Annette's lower lip trembled, and the little tremors would not stop.

Cole's eyes were steel gray. "I think we got another mountain lion, judging from the size. To see him from here, he must be three hundred pounds. I think he might be interested in my cattle in the meadow." Cole looked at Annette.

"They've come down before at this time of year. I took care of them before and I can take care of them again. Please stay inside with the windows and doors closed today. Don't even go to the barn or the pump. There are a couple of buckets of water inside by the back door." Cole smiled trying to relieve her fear. "You'll be safe in the house."

Annette sensed the danger of the situation and wrapped her arms around him and hugged him hard. "When will you be back?"

Cole placed his free hand on the small of her back and held her tight. He buried his face in her hair. "I'll be back when I get him or by dark, whichever is first. I won't track him in the dark. Cats are nocturnal and have the advantage then."

He closed the heavy wooden door securely behind him and went to the barn behind the mama cat who held the last one of her kittens securely by the nape of its neck. Once inside he counted the kittens and closed the large barn door. He made sure there were no kittens left outside and saddled the fastest horse.

He placed the Sharp's rifle in the scabbard and packed extra ammo in the saddle bag along with his sharpest hunting knives. He opened the door and led the animal outside, then made sure it was shut and bolted securely. Then he mounted up and rode down the road.

Annette watched him ride away on one of the racing horses and decided to get a better view from the loft window. She climbed the ladder and pressed herself against the window pane watching Cole fade in the distance. Then she realized how big the animal she saw was in comparison to Cole's size and her fear grew. She watched for a long while but could not see anything else. She climbed back down the ladder and went to the kitchen.

Annette cleared away the fried chicken meant for lunch and wrapped the biscuits in a towel to keep them from drying out. She made some coffee and went to get Cole's almanac from last year. She began reading trying to find references to last year's problem with the big cats.

It was the longest day of her life until she heard hooves against the hard dirt of the road late in afternoon and raced to the window. Cole rode in with a couple of animal skins hanging on the back of his horse. She ran to the door ready to unbolt the latch, waiting to hear Cole's voice.

"Annette, come out and see what I've got."

She unbolted the heavy door. Cole sat grinning on the horse and patted the yellow gold skins draped over the black horse's hindquarters.

"Got two mountain lions this time," he said with pride.

Annette was speechless when tears welled in her eyes. She realized she did not need to be fearful for him. "Oh, my, they must have been huge judging from the size of the skins. What will you do with them?" She wiped her eyes with the corner of her apron.

"Come on, I'll show you." Cole noticed tears on her cheeks but could not touch her face and wipe them away. Blood and guts from the task of skinning the two big cats, covered his body. The largest of the cats weighed three hundred pounds and the smaller around two hundred.

Annette walked to the side of the barn and saw two skins tacked down to the barn wood.

He pointed to the two skins tacked onto the barn wood. "I'll take those both down since the curing process is complete and tack these two new ones up in their places. Guess I'll roll up the cured ones and store them in the barn."

Annette reached up, brushed the silken hair on the dried skin. "Instead of rolling them up, can you roll them both out in front of the fireplace for the winter?"

"Don't see why not. They might look nice."
Cole felt happy she thought enough of his trophies to
want them in the cabin. He finished unloading the
skins from his horse and tacked the two new ones on
the barn wall.

Cole cleaned up in the barn before going to
the cabin. He stripped down and rinsed with a
bucket of cold water, then lathered up with homemade lye soap and rinsed with more buckets of cold
water. He toweled off and slipped into his deerskin
pants. He made a dead sprint to the cabin when the
wind changed directions from the south west to the
north with bitter cold gusts. He bounded into the
cabin. "I think we're in for some weather tonight."

"Where's your shirt and shoes?"

"Decided to wash up instead of going back out
there and didn't have anything except my deer-
skins." He stood in front of the stove and warmed
himself rubbing his hands across his chest.

"Let me measure you for your shirts, and then
you can finish getting dressed." She already set the
table for the evening meal and went to retrieve her
sewing box. She took great care in measuring his
chest. She wanted to get the shirts perfect. He
smelled of clean soap and leather and she struggled
to concentrate on her task.

Cole had added at least two inches to his
chest since she began cooking for him, but his waist
measurement stayed the same. He looked healthier
than he did when they met the first day on the prairie, when she felt sure his ribs were sticking out under his shirt.

"What kind of weather are we in for?" She

69

asked while pulling the measuring tape across his chest.

"Maybe some freezing rain or snow. One never knows in this country, but you can be sure the weather will be different than the day before."

When Annette finished measuring, Cole stood still for a minute not wanting to leave her proximity, then he stepped back and threw a couple of logs into the fireplace. He grabbed an undershirt from his bureau and wrote something down in the almanac.

"Can I find out what I'm supposed to be doing in this marriage since we know about your duties?" They read the second part of the chapter and she knew she would have no problem with the honor and respect passage. She pointed to the 'obey' portion of scripture and felt the hair on her neck prickle at the thought.

"I can certainly honor you and respect your decisions. You are strong and protective of me and you have only shown me kindness since I came here. But I should be honest about this part. I'm pretty strong willed and have my own opinions about things."

"Yep, woman, I know ya got ears and a right smart brain between 'em," he mocked himself and smiled at her, remembering his words the day they first met.

"Yep, I got ears, and my name is Annette."

"Little did I know. I'll never speak to you again in a disrespectful manner. You didn't deserve my words. I won't be ordering you around," he promised.

Annette looked at him for a full minute, then said, "Tell me about prayer."

Cole looked puzzled. "What do you mean?"

"Is a prayer only when you bow your head and fold your hands and talk to God or is a prayer even when you think aloud or whisper when no one's around?"

"A prayer is anytime you ask God for anything or talk to Him. When you address Him silently or in a whisper when no one is around, they all count as prayer and God answers prayers. Sometimes He answers them before you ask them. He already knows what's in your heart."

~ * ~

Annette enjoyed the warmth of the fire during her bath behind the curtain. She thought about the day she met Cole at the graveside. Only moments before she whispered what she thought might be her first prayer when she asked God, "What am I to do?"

She reviewed the rush of feelings building inside of her during the day. First, fear for him then relief and finally, she was simply proud of him. She counted each memory from the day they hunted turkey in the grove, the shooting lessons, and the rides they took together in the late afternoons. She could feel his breathe in her hair, and his hands on her waist, and the pressure of her body against his when she fired the gun.

Annette knew she felt attracted to him since the first day when he pulled her up from where she sat on the sod. However, she felt attracted to someone before. Tony did not care for her safety, for her well-being, for her daily needs, and most of all, he

71

did not return her deep feelings. Tony took what he wanted when convenient for him with no thought for her.

Her feelings for Tony diminished every day they were together with the strongest attraction being the day she left the Palace to run off with him. She also knew she used Tony for her escape from a life and a future she did not want. She realized they were both guilty of selfish behavior.

Cole was different from any other man and she knew she loved him. Those feelings were growing every day since the first day they met. She knew they shared feelings involving the future, not only the moment in which they lived. Annette knew she would stay with him when they returned from Mud Creek in the spring. She must know if he felt the same way.

She toweled off and dressed in her finest chemise. This time she did not put on her housedress. She turned off the lamp, crossed the room and stood on the skin rug in front of the fireplace. The flames cast a golden red glow on her.

Cole looked up from where he sat on the bed when he saw her in the firelight. She simply stood there with huge brown eyes and the palest of skin. He got up and went to see what she needed.

She looked up at him. "Do you love me, Cole?"

"More than anything on this earth, I love you." He placed his arms around her pulling her to him. "Do you love me, Annette?" He whispered and swept her into his arms.

"More than anything on this earth, I love

you."

~Seven~

Love in God's Eyes

*A*nnette awakened in the dim morning light. The cabin felt shivering cold and she pulled the heavy quilt closer around her shoulders and nestled against Cole's chest. Then she sat upright in bed, shocked for a second before Cole pulled her to him and she remembered the night before.

"Let me start the fire before you get up." He dressed and began moving logs into the fireplace.

They were both surprised to see gray skies and white snowflakes flying across the windows. Cole rekindled the fire in the fireplace and Annette dressed and went to the stove to get coffee ready.

Cole pulled his watch from the pocket of his jacket. "Wow, mid-morning."

"There's no way, the sun's not up yet," Annette said.

"Oh, the sun's up, just blocked by the snowfall." Cole grabbed his heaviest coat from the peg by the door. "I'll be back in about fifteen minutes. I need to make sure the cattle haven't busted down the corral and see what else I need to do today."

Cole grabbed a long length of rope hanging next to the back door and tied the end securely around the back-porch post. Annette watched in wonder when he moved with the other end of the rope in hand toward the corral. His form disappeared only a few steps out and Annette realized the snow blew sideways and blinded visibility past a few feet.

Bare patches of brown dirt dotted the ground, surrounded by swirling snow and small drifts formed
around the front porch columns and the rocker. Cole
reappeared in about fifteen minutes and stomped
the snow from his boots on the back porch.

They drank coffee and talked while the oatmeal simmered. "I tied the rope in a triangle. I'll
draw the diagram for you in case you need to go outside. The long side of the triangle reaches from the
back-porch to the outhouse, and then to the corral.
The two short sides go from the corral to the barn,
and the barn to the front porch directly in front of
the rocker." He traced out the pattern on a piece of
paper and labeled the buildings.

"If you go out, never let go of the rope or you
could freeze to death before you get back inside.
When I go to the barn this afternoon, you can go too
so you know what the blizzard feels like."

Annette agreed but found herself a little
frightened by this new territory's winter howling
outside. "Is snow out here always like this?"

"Not always. Sometimes snow is soft and deep
but when the wind blows, snow is plain wicked.
Doesn't take much more than a few inches to make a
drift with wind like we get. What's snow like back in
New Orleans? I don't suppose snow ever fell in New
Orleans?"

"Once huge white flakes came down. The
snow lasted only a few minutes and melted after the
flakes touched the ground. One year I went to
boarding school in Boston. The snow swirled into
large drifts, wet and deep. The rest of the time, my
mother sent me to a school in Virginia. There was no

snow there."

They spent the rest of the morning talking about their childhoods and comparing their pasts. Each comparison helped them push forward in their relationship.

At noon, Cole bundled her up like a mom getting her child ready to go out and play in the snow. They inched their way along the rope from the front porch pillar to the barn and could barely see each other and their own hands when the wind gusts blew the fresh snow all around them.

Cole closed the barn doors and held her close. "See what I mean about the ropes?"

"Oh, goodness, yes. One could surely die if you let go. I almost died hanging on to the rope."

Annette's body shook not so much from the cold, but from the prospect of losing Cole in the weather raging outside. Twice Annette had not been able to see more than a few inches from her face. A deep fear of being in something she could not get out of overcame her. She had stopped walking but did not let go of the rope until the fear began to recede. Her breathing all but stopped when she had not been able to see her hand in front of her face and she felt encapsulated in the snow. When the gust slowed, she could see again and began to breathe.

"If you should ever fall or let go, wait a second, stand up and reach out for the rope but don't step out. You may have to turn a circle to find the rope, but don't step out."

"I'm not going out without you."

Cole tied a rope around a large shock of hay.

"I'm going to drag this out to the corral while you pet those kittens. This could take me thirty minutes or more, so stay in the barn."

The kittens would only allow a few minutes of petting and they were off on a hunt on the far side of the barn. They shied away from the doors when they were open and huddled with the mother cat behind a bale of hay.

Annette walked around the inside of the barn and up the stairs to the loft several times to get some exercise when she heard Cole push the barn door open. She peered over the railing of the loft to make sure she could count all the kittens before he closed the door. She thought she could see panic on Cole's face when he searched the main floor and didn't find her.

"I'm up here," she called and saw relief flood his face.

He bounded up the stairs. "Come with me. There's something I want to show you." He led Annette over to the eaves on the west side of the barn. He shed his jacket and laid the garment on the loose hay. Cole lifted a board and reached inside.

Cole laid a small gun on his jacket and then deposited a few more items from the space, including a stack of bills, a small leather bag, and a white kerchief tied up by the corners. He opened the kerchief and spilled several pieces of jewelry onto the jacket with the other contents.

Annette starred at the cache of valuables and her eyes grew wide when she saw Tony's derringer. "What is all this? Where did you get these items? I recognize Tony's derringer. I thought the derringer must still be in his inside jacket pocket when they buried him."

"We didn't bury any derringer with Tony. When we prepared him for burial, we checked every pocket and they were all empty. The derringer lay hidden in a compartment in your wagon." He paused for a moment.

"These items are all yours. I found the cache the first day I brought you home and hid everything up here for safe keeping until I thought the time would be right to bring them out. There are several more bundles of cash like this one." He pointed to the cash bundle tied with string but could not look her in the face, ashamed he waited to tell her about the items.

"Why did you wait so long?" Annette reached up and cupped his face.

"I thought you would leave if you knew you had the resources to go and I didn't want to give you up, even from the first minute we met. I'm sorry, I didn't have a right to hide the items." There were tears in his eyes waiting to spill over. "Are you going to leave this spring when the weather allows us to travel to Mud Creek?"

She rubbed his cold cheeks with her warm hands, wiping a single tear. "I'll never leave you. I'm in love with you."

"Are you mad at me for keeping this from you?"

"No. Well, maybe a little. We must never keep anything from each other. Did you think I knew about all this?"

"At first, I didn't know, but when I got to

know you I realized you couldn't have known about these items. I realized you would never take anything that wasn't yours. Initials are engraved on the back of several jewelry pieces, so I knew they weren't yours or Tony's." Cole picked up one of the pieces and turned it over in his hand. A set of initials, EWF, engraved in elaborate fashion, ran across the back of the necklace.

Annette shook her head. "The only thing I recognize is Tony's gun. He ran back to the wagon one night in Kansas City saying some sore losers were upset about the card game and he outran them. I knew he lied to me again. I could always tell when he lied to me, but I didn't know why until this moment. His pockets were bulging with something and he went to sleep wearing his coat.

I think he stole all this in Kansas City. I remember smelling gunpowder on him and I moved to the front of the wagon to sleep for the night. When I woke up at dawn we were already moving past the feed yards on the outskirts of town.

The jewelry and money are not ours and not Tony's either, except for the derringer. I am sure all the jewelry belongs to someone else. Let's take this inside. I want to catalog everything in a list and write a letter to the sheriff in Kansas City."

Cole packed the cache back into the box and wondered if she might be mistaken about the derringer. Annette could not have seen this derringer since it was under a heavy trunk in a hidden compartment. Yet she said Tony kept it in his coat pocket. When the men prepared his body for burial, they found no money, no guns, no pocket watch, or anything thing else in his jacket.

Annette starred at the box quietly for a long minute and finally said, "I can't imagine what you must have thought of me at first. Traveling, unmarried with a man and then hearing about where I grew up and who my mother was. I ran the very first chance I got and count myself lucky to have come to this place where you are. I am a tainted wom—"

Cole reached out to touch her face and ran his thumb over her lips abruptly silencing her words. "You are perfect and all I ever dared to hope for. I believe God's will brought you here, not luck."

~ * ~

By the next afternoon, the snow stopped. Most of the snow piled up against the out buildings and cabin and left bare brown patches of earth on the ground. The dry snow resisted the full sunshine of the afternoon for several days, then finally melted into muddy puddles that kept refreezing at night. The moisture lasted only a few days and they were back to cold, dry, windy days with sunshine in the afternoons.

"Cole can you pull in the chairs and the sofa a little closer to the fireplace and center the furniture on the rugs?" Annette asked. She placed supper in the oven to slow cook and sat down with the almanac to see how many days until Christmas. She counted them off at twenty-one days to finish his shirts. She worked on them every day when he went out to feed the animals. With only the buttons and button holes left to do, she would complete the task on time.

Annette decided to work on her letter to the Kansas City sheriff and got the letter out of the sewing box. The letter to her mother lay at the bottom of the stack, unfinished. Cole told her the Pony Express should come through in a couple of weeks and she should go ahead and get the letter ready.

She listed the contents Cole discovered in the wagon and told the sheriff she suspected Tony stole them. She wrote down what the initials were and asked for help in returning the items to their rightful owner. She gave Tony's full name and his physical description, the date of his death, and the date Cole found the items hidden in the wagon. She included an exact cash amount.

She described the night in Kansas City with an approximate date of Tony's story about the sore losers and the card game. Annette also wrote she lived with her husband, Cole Waldren, and noted a description of their land location, west and south of the abandoned Fort Atkinson in the Kansas Territory. Finally, she sealed the letter in an envelope and set it on the mantel.

~ * ~

After lunch, they mounted two of the horses, with Cole on the larger one named Midnight and Annette on the smaller brown one named Dawn. With two days in the barn, the horses were ready to run.

After a brief warm up around the barn and corrals, Cole gave Midnight the lead. He looked back, surprised to see Annette and Dawn only a step behind to his left. She leaned forward in the saddle and Dawn gained ground on Midnight. The race continued neck and neck until both horses were tired and began to slow. Finally, they slowed the animals to a walk.

At a grove of trees, they dismounted to let the horses rest. They found a small pool of melting snow in one of the limestone rocks for the horses to drink, and spent a lazy afternoon sitting on the large limestone boulders enjoying the sun.

Cole told her about his plans for a new house. Annette listened in amazement when Cole described what he wanted to build out of the limestone which made up the hill behind the cabin where boulders strewn about the grove were big enough for stone blocks. Cole told her he saw some limestone construction north of Mud Creek and sent for information about how to cut the stones.

"I watched the men driving long metal stakes into the limestone at twelve-inch intervals. They simply drive stakes at the edges of whatever shape they wanted the block to be and the soft yellow limestone came off the main rock in neat rectangular shapes. They stacked the blocks together outlining the structure and the house took shape."

"Where would you build this house?"

"Wherever on the land you want."

Annette appeared speechless and starred at Cole with a gaping mouth.

"I don't think I've ever seen you speechless," he laughed.

"Won't you need help? You can't do heavy work without help. In addition, building will take a hefty sum of money for labor, lumber, and roofing materials. Where will all the construction materials come from? When do you plan to do this? And where are the sites I can choose from?" Annette took a gulp of air to keep going and Cole laughed until there were tears in his eyes.

"There's my Annette. Let's ride back a different way than we came, and I'll show you some of the land you haven't seen yet."

They rode for several miles to areas where hills backed up to draws and meadows with streams of clear water. There were cliffs of limestone overhanging sheltered areas like the one behind the cabin. The trees were mostly cottonwood and cedar scattered about against the cliffs. The front part of Cole's property, covered in flat grasslands, left her wondering why the cabin wasn't nestled back in the trees or by a creek.

They watered the horses again at a stream. "Any of the meadow areas would offer a level building surface and protection from the elements," Cole said. "I have enough money to bring in workers and skilled stonecutters for construction."

"You don't live like you've got a lot of money. Your shirts are threadbare and there's nothing excessive about your lifestyle."

"Most of what I have, I've earned in the last few years from my cattle. I've banked every bit of the money in an account in Mud Creek. Each year, I keep out only enough for feed and supplies and increase the size of my herd. Someday we will get more for our cattle when we can sell directly at the railhead instead of selling to cattle buyers at the pens. Mud Creek will have a railhead someday. Timothy Hersey has plans drawn out and his wife wants to name it Abilene.

"Let's go back. I want to show you where I keep the bank books."

They mounted up and galloped back to the barn. Darkness overtook them and by the time they reached the barn, the horses were ready for feed and water. Annette helped rub the animals down and hung the bridles up while Cole brought water in from the pump. All four of the animals looked healthy under Cole's care.

Annette patted Midnight's ribs. "They're filling out nicely and seem to be healthier than when you got them."

"Kind of like me." Cole patted his rib cage and laughed.

Annette took the opportunity to place her hands on his chest, tracing the outlines of his muscles with her fingers. "Yep, you've filled out right nice, mister."

Cole's throat went dry and he could not even think of the reason they came into the barn. Finally, he grabbed her hands so he could think. He held them and led her to the steps up to the loft.

Once up the stairs, he went to the eaves and lifted the boards where he stored the cache from the wagon and pulled out a leather-bound ledger. He opened the ledger on a bale of hay.

"This is a record of my deposits for the last few years at the bank in Mud Creek."

The last deposit was dated the previous April, and the total at the bottom of the page was large. Annette kept ledger totals for her mother and the totals were never this large.

"If anything should ever happen to me, you are to take this to the bank in Mud Creek. I have a letter ready for the pony express rider adding you to the account." Cole looked into Annette's eyes. "Money is only a tool we use to take care of our family and to help those less fortunate than we are. God gives resources to us to use and care for, but they are not ours, everything is His, we are only His stewards. I will show you in the Bible where the information about stewardship is written when we read tonight." He closed the ledger and placed it back in the space in the eaves.

Annette knew he truly believed every word he said.

~ * ~

During the Bible reading Annette asked, "Have you ever read the entire Bible from front to back?"

"The winter after my folks died, I started reading from the beginning. I watched my mother read in the evenings, so I picked up the book and started. She taught us all to read by using the easiest of the verses. But when I read the longer verses, they gave me some trouble. I wished I paid more attention and been a better student. I finally finished in the spring and started reading over again. I've gone through the book twice, and I go back to look up some of the things when I have questions."

"You've been here all by yourself since your folks died?"

"For a couple of years. My brothers left within a few weeks and I have not seen them since. When I got lonely, I remembered God must have a plan for me, I only needed to wait things out, and then you came."

"Why didn't you marry Ellie? I saw the look she gave me on our wedding day. I no doubt upset her plans."

"Her plans were not my plans. I don't think her heart is in the right place. There are plenty of examples in the Bible about women who think and act like she does. Enough talk about Ellie. Can we put the lamp out?"

Annette turned the lamp down until the flame went out.

~Eight~
Christmas

Only two days left until Christmas and Annette finished the last buttons on Cole's new shirts. For the project, she took apart one of her dresses with a plain geometric print and saved the buttons from the threadbare shirts she used for patterns. She placed the finished shirts in some of the store tissue wrap from her dresses and found a string to tie the package together.

She made four shirts in all and knew Cole needed them. He worked on something in the barn for several days and she suspected he labored over her Christmas present.

Annette remembered the Christmas's at the Palace and the extravagant gifts her mother bestowed on her—a piano, a rosewood four-poster bed, and mounds of clothing from Paris and London designed especially for her. However, there was never a celebration centered on the birth of the baby Jesus. They enjoyed eggnog, a variety of foods, and gifts from numerous guests. Her mother even set up a small tree in the main room and hung brightly colored decorations from France. Beautifully wrapped gifts were placed under the tree for all the girls, the servants, and for Annette.

Magnolia once told her Christmas is to celebrate the baby Jesus' birthday, but Annette never heard the story read from the Bible. Annette's

mother did not allow Bibles at the Palace and si-
lenced Magnolia when she began to talk about the
virgin birth. Annette accepted her mother's direction but knew this deeply saddened Magnolia.

Annette placed the tissue wrapped package in
her trunk beside the fireplace before Cole came in
from the barn. With no warning, she barely got the
package stowed away.
Cole butchered one of the smaller cows from
the herd and there were fine lean cuts of beef to
eat. He rebuilt a large cold-box in the earth next to
the stream and filled it with butchered beef.
Annette planned to cook a roast on Christmas
day with potatoes and brown gravy, fresh bread and
butter, and white Christmas cake in honor of the
baby Jesus' birthday. She also found a jar of pickles
and one of tiny pickled corn in the pantry and
guarded them for just such a special occasion.

"Would you like to go for a ride today?" Cole
asked when he came in and set two large bundles on
the table. "I have to run an errand to the Smith
homestead and then the Wilks' place, and we need
to start early if we want to be back by dark."
"I'd love to ride today. What are the er-
rands?"
"I want to take them each a part of the beef I
butchered as Christmas gifts." He motioned to the
two large bundles of meat on the table. "They've
been good neighbors and I'd like to share with them.
I think the Wilks' are having a rough time of things
lately."

Annette grabbed her heavy sweater and Cole helped her button it securely around her small frame. She then layered her riding jacket on top and finally one of Cole's older, smaller leather jackets on top. She felt like a child bundling up for playtime in the snow, but she knew with the wind, every layer would be necessary. Cole bundled up too, and they were off to the barn to get two of the horses.

With a beautiful morning, the horses covered the distance to the Smith farmstead at a fast trot. Tom and Georgia came out to greet them and they gathered in the kitchen for hot tea and pie. The Smiths were grateful for the meat and thanked Cole and Annette many times.

"Where did the apples came from for the pie?" Annette asked.

"The harvest was plentiful this year. I canned most of the crop for use later to bake pies. Tom brought the trees all the way from Pennsylvania when we settled here. We planted them when we first arrived, and they seemed to adapt to the prairie sod. I will save you some of the largest seeds for planting next year when we harvest."

"Thank you," Annette exclaimed in delight when Georgia produced two jars of canned apples for their Christmas present.

An hour later, Cole stashed the canned goods in his saddlebags and they mounted up and set out for the Wilks' place. Annette did not know what to expect when they rode up to a shabby structure.

"This is the Wilks homestead," Cole said.

Annette would have called the structure a shack and noted the barn appeared to be much nicer and had a second story. With two large doors atop the lower barn doors, it loomed over the bare yard. A pulley mounted over the doors puzzled Annette and she wondered what it was there for.

Cole saw her looking at the structure. "John wants to raise cotton out here and someday he'll get around to planting the crop. The pulley system is to move large cotton bales to the upper floor for dry storage."

"Cotton?" Annette asked. "They have cotton east of New Orleans. Is the weather warm enough here for cotton?"

"John maintains if you planted the cotton early enough without it freezing out, the crop would work. He might be right."

"I am right," John said, coming out of the barn. "I've got seed coming in the spring and I'm going to give things a try. What are you two doing out in the cold today?"

"I hope the crop works for you, John. We're out delivering Christmas presents and have a bundle of beef for you that we butchered. I wanted to share the bounty."

"Why thank you. We can truly use the meat." John shook Cole's hand and looked back at the cabin. "Ellie's not up to coming out, but I know she'll appreciate beef instead of chicken for a change." John said thanks again and walked back to his shabby cabin without inviting them in.

Annette starred at the cabin, looking at Ellie, who watched through a window, and she could see dark circles under Ellie's eyes. "She looks like she gained weight."

"Let's go," Cole said, and they backed the horses for a couple of steps out of the yard, and then turned the animals toward their cabin.

"Sarah, John's wife, died on Ellie's twelfth birthday. John takes a hauling job or odd work when they need money and is gone for weeks at a time," Cole explained. "Ellie's always been left to handle everything around the place when John is gone. I sure hope he gets his cotton planted this spring."

Annette listened intently and finally decided she heard enough about Ellie. "Race you for a mile."

Cole nodded, and she rode off at break-neck speed. Annette leaned forward in the saddle, edging her horse on when Cole saw the fence rail at the edge of the Wilks' property. Horrified, he watched Annette's horse approach the rail at a dead run. She bent low over the horse's neck, talking softly to the mare and when the moment came, she made a quick movement with the bridle and the horse jumped the rail with ease. Annette slowed and let Cole catch up.

"What in the name of Heaven are you doing?"

"Jumping." Annette smile. "We've been prac- ticing when we can, and she loves jumping as much as I do."

Annette could see anger and fear on Cole's face, making it appear red and blotchy. "I'm a trained horse woman, Cole. I know how to jump and have won competitions back east. Dawn is perfect for jumping and she trained easily. Don't worry, I'm not in any danger and I know what I'm doing," she concluded firmly.

Cole starred at her in disbelief. He knew she could tell he did not like her jumping and thought the practice too dangerous, but Annette simply ignored him. She even smiled, obviously having fun with the ride.

They finished the ride home in complete silence and rubbed the horses down. "I still think jumping is a dangerous thing to do and don't want you doing it," Cole said.

Annette looked at him. "No, I won't stop. I don't see a reason to stop. I feel I'm safe, so I will continue to jump until one or the other of us, patting Dawn, is pregnant and should not jump."

When he found himself alone in the barn, he decided he did hear the firm 'no' and sat on a bale of straw to think. "What is she thinking? Everything is going perfectly and suddenly she's got her own mind about things?"

Yes, she does have her own mind about things and should have. I knew that the first day I met her. I cannot command her like a child who needs directing, and I cannot tell her what she should think or do.

Cole sat for long time thinking about what Annette said. He knew she left the safety of her mother's house because she did not want someone else deciding what the rest of her life would hold for her. He remembered when he ordered his younger brothers around after his folks died. They did not like his commands either, and soon, they were gone. They left to make their own lives somewhere else, somewhere away from him. Cole knew he could not live without Annette and would simply die if she left him.

He must let go of this need to control people

and activities and let them decide their own lives. He kept going back over his Bible readings and understood what the Lord said and what He did not say. He did not say woman should be man's slave. He said helpmate, not galley maid. He said partner, walking beside not behind, taken from a man's side to walk at his side.

He knew her presence in his life to be a gift from God and they should care for each other's needs. Annette let him know she liked to race and jump horses even though he could not understand.

"Alright Lord. I'll give this another shot and try to listen to her needs."

~Nine~
Ellie

Ellie sat in the opening of the second story barn doors with her feet dangling over the edge. The open doors allowed cool air to rush in and move her bangs away from her clammy forehead. Against the clear blue sky, the sun beamed down intense and direct.

"I found a few days' work for a farmer east of here," John told her the day he left. "Don't worry about me if things take longer before I'm back, got lots to do." She knew he would be gone at least a week or two.

John made a habit of leaving after her mother died. He said they made their living with his odd jobs and he always came back with money, and sometimes he brought gifts for her like the new calico dress hanging in her closet. She wondered where John got the items. He never left long enough to make the trip to the marketplace in Mud Creek. She suspected he stole items regularly with no idea how far out he rode on his trips to glean supplies from wherever he found them.

Ellie wore the new calico dress when she went on a picnic near the stream with Bobby Smith during the summer months. Bobby traveled to the territory from the gulf coast to work for his older brother, Tom.

"I worked on the docks on the gulf coast loading and unloading ships near Shreveport," Bobby said. "When I fell in with bad friends and got into trouble, my mother sent me away to hide from the law out here to Tom's place. I plan to stay and work long enough to save some money and pay for a horse, so I can go to Kansas City and start over."

She packed them a lunch of fried chicken and buttered bread sandwiches and pickles. She hoped to leave with Bobby and he promised she could go with him to Kansas City. Then one morning, like John, Bobby left the territory.

Before her father left, they were not eating much of anything, only a few root vegetables she dug up in the garden, some beans, and the last slices of bread. Ellie felt relief to see Cole and Annette ride up one morning and leave a nice bundle of beef.

Her throat felt sore, and she felt unusually warm, not even wearing a shawl outside. The cool air coming in the second story barn doors felt good. She felt the glands on both sides of her throat that had swelled out to lumps. She used her finger to trace the red blotches running up her left arm. The limb felt very stiff.

She suffered a puncture wound on her left hand from a fall she took a few days ago. She landed on an upturned sharp stick that poked deep into her hand and it was now swollen and sore. She felt like she could not open her jaws and yawn.

She placed her hand on her barely rounded belly and stood. She remembered when she fell from this very spot at only twelve years of age. The fall hurt badly but at least she did not break any bones. No one ever knew she accidently fell out of the barn

95

after her mother died.

John had been gone a week and no one came around to check on her, so she simply laid down for a day or two with aches and pains and returned to her normal life afterwards. She never mentioned the incident to anyone.

She stepped backwards, not wanting to be near the edge. A pain gripped her abdomen and she bent over to ease the contraction. The pain stopped suddenly, so she climbed down the ladder, and started toward the cabin. Before she got to the porch, the next pain came. Ellie steadied herself against the porch railing and then went into the house and sat on the edge of the bed.

Terror gripped her. *This is much too early, only four months maybe.* She knew the child inside her belly would come too soon.

~ * ~

Cole finished the small rack for Annette's Christmas present. He placed the final round spindle in the hole and tapped the last peg into place. The rack would be perfect for her collection of threads and sported a special set of spindles to hang her scissors from with a charcoal outline of the scissors around the spot. Cole made the rack from a piece of walnut he saved for a special project. He rubbed the rack by hand with Tung oil to make a smooth finish. He held his work up to the light and decided the thread rack looked complete.

He held the prize tight to his chest and prayed Annette would like his work. The weather felt strangely warmer than usual this afternoon and he opened the barn to air out the musty smell of animals and hay. He could feel the cold coming in across the plains from the north when evening drew in.

Might be snow coming again. Snow would be perfect for Christmas morning. He smiled and grabbed a dusty bottle from under a feed bin. He tucked this prize under his arm and secured the barn doors.

Annette set out an array of what Magnolia called finger foods across the large table and placed small plates at the end of the table beside the bounty. There were chicken wings brushed with a sauce made of tomato paste, vinegar, and hot peppers, deer sausage and cheese slices, small flakey apple pies baked in the cupcake pan, an array of sugar cookies, and beef strips cooked with cabbage then wrapped in small squares of raised yeast bread and baked to a golden brown. She also made a pot of hot tea and added honey.

Cole came in and stopped abruptly at the table. "I've never seen anything like this."

"This is what we used to do at the Palace," Annette said and motioned down the length of the table full of bite-sized goodies. "We were allowed to take plates of food and sit in front of the fireplace and go back for more whenever we wanted." She paused and tried to see what he was hiding. "What is in the bottle you've got tucked under your arm? And what's behind your back?"

Cole set the dusty bottle of wine on the table with one hand and pulled the thread rack out from behind his back with the other.

Annette giggled in delight. "This is perfect." She touched the sleek, finely grained wood. "For my threads and even a place for my scissors. Thank you."

They ate on the sofa in front of the fireplace and went back for second helpings. Cole got his Bible and they read the Christmas story together. It was the first time Annette had heard the story of the first Christmas read from the Bible, and she sat quietly, contemplating the Virgin Mary giving birth in a stable.

Annette felt more than a little afraid at the prospect of giving birth here in the middle of nowhere whenever her time came. She took a moment and prayed whenever a pregnancy might happen, the baby would be safe and healthy, and she would find the strength like Mary.

Suddenly, she remembered her gift for Cole and jumped up to get the package of shirts out of her trunk. Cole closed his book and took the package with a smile. When he opened the gift, he noticed the green fabric from her dress, the one he chose for her to wear the first day they were man and wife.

He marveled at the ability with which she fashioned such fine shirts for him. The masculine print with straight lines and small squares of different shades of green, looked to be far fancier than a work shirt. "This is from the dress you wore that first day we were man and wife. I will always associate the day with this shirt."

The other shirts were a plain, solid gray color from the servant's dress she wore the first day they met at Tony's funeral. They were meant for everyday wear but still displayed perfect workmanship.

"I've never owned such fine things. Thank you, Annette. What beautiful work you do with your hands."

Cole opened the wine. "This wine is from a batch my parents made for the barn raising several years ago, and everyone who helped enjoyed a large glass full of the elderberry wine. I watched my dad hide one last bottle in the barn under a feed bin and knew someday there would be an occasion for this." He poured each of them a glass full of the aged wine and they enjoyed the firelight until well after midnight.

~ * ~

Ellie watched the sun set through the empty front window and poured another glass of water. She felt a bit stronger and decided to clean up in the washtub next to the stove. She lit a fire and began stripping down, depositing the soiled garments in a pile in a second empty tub. She washed, then dressed in an old clean shirt. She turned the lamp wick down until the flame went out and lay on her small cot waiting for sleep to overtake her.

Hours passed, and she starred at the flames in the old iron stove, but sleep would not come. Her stomach was flat. She buried the tiny fetus in her garden and marked the spot with a small cross. She dug the grave using her sore swollen hand to press against the handle of the shovel. A sharp piece of metal on the shovel handle tore a small hole in her sore hand. The pain gave way a little when blood and infection began to leak out of the hole in her hand. She soaked her hand in hot Epsom salts water, not even noticing the pain. Her heart hurt far greater.

"Did you take my baby for punishment, God?" She cried out, hating the entire world.

She finally drifted into a deep sleep even though the wind whistled through the cracks in the walls of the shack. She dreamed about warm sunshine, eating all the food she wanted and suddenly, she heard her mother speak to her.

At first, she thought the vision must be a dream, but she opened her eyes and starred into the fire. Then Ellie sat up on the edge of the bed, eyes open, still starring at the fire and she knew she heard her mother talking. She listened intently to the story her mother read. She used to listen when her mother read aloud from the rocking chair, glued to every word.

The story told about a girl who sewed in a factory in the south somewhere. The girl left her home at an early age to make her own way in the world, sleeping where she could, eating what she could find and finally, saving enough coins to rent a room where she would be safe from the world.

For an instant, she thought she saw the rocker by the stove move. Terrified, she thought she saw a ghost and she wept with fear until she lost herself again in fitful sleep. When she slept, her sore hand hung over the edge of bed onto the cold floor, infection and blood draining down the rough wooden planks.

~ * ~

Cole sat at the kitchen table with the bright winter sunlight streaming in through the clean glass windows. Annette sat beside him, and they looked at his journal dated back to the spring of last year.

"We all drive whatever livestock we have ready to sell to the pens near Mud Creek each spring. We sell cattle and horses to buyers from Kansas City. The buyers then drive the herds to the railhead at Kansas City for shipping. My brothers and I always made the trip with our folks. When it came to farming, it was the only thing my brothers were excited about each year."

"I think the Kansas Pacific Railroad may extend their line to Mud Creek soon. The newspapers are all writing about an expansion of the rail spur. Most of this part of the territory makes the journey in late March, or early April when the weather allows, and sell off their herds. Some bank their money, and some spend in the local saloon, but everyone needs to restock supplies with no stores west of Mud Creek."

"My parents drew up careful detailed lists of supplies. They planned menus and livestock feed rations had to be calculated out for a full year. They changed their lists many times before they considered them perfect."

Cole's building projects were drawn out with detailed, exact calculations and topped the stack of lists. "Do you want to travel with me for the trip? We could be gone four to six weeks and I'm not comfortable leaving you here without protection."

He did not want to order her to go but staying behind alone could be dangerous. "There will be a contingent of troops accompanying us to make sure no Indians take strays from our herds."

"Indians?"

"I've never experienced any trouble with them, but they are around this area at various times depending on how their food supply holds out. Sometimes they come from the western edge of the mountains looking for food. I usually cut out a couple of cattle from the herd and make a gift to them. They were here over a year ago, and we set out by the barn on the side where the skins are pegged out. They seemed to like to look at the skins and began calling me a warrior. Their warriors also take the mountain lions for their skins and consider the wearing of the pelts a great honor. I gave their chieftain one and he swore his protection for me and my family forever. There's no need to fear them."

Annette, wide-eyed and full of questions about the Indians, kept interrupting and Cole kept leading back to the task of list-making. Finally, Annette knew her questions would have to wait.

"Could we take your covered wagon this year instead of only horses?" Cole asked.

"Yes, *our* wagon," Annette corrected him with a smile.

Cole smiled and nodded. "Yes, I think I'd like the protection of the canvas instead of an open-air bed on the ground. I'll get the wagon ready."

He felt excited at the prospect of showing Annette the new settlement of Mud Creek. "They've got a couple of general stores and a nice boarding house. There's talk about starting a hotel by spring." His smile faded. "The stage should make a run back to Kansas City this spring."

Annette understood his fears. She knew he still felt insecure and thought she might leave if given a chance. She looked into his eyes. "I'll never leave your side, Cole. You've become a part of me and I couldn't bear to think of a day without you."

Cole's dark expression faded, and he smiled again. "Nor I."

They planned the trip starting with the lists building excitement each day.

~ * ~

The winter days passed quietly and swiftly. The only visitor was the pony express rider and after his pick-up of their mail, he was gone as quickly as he arrived. The pair became closer and planned their future, starting with supplies and livestock. Cole planned more slotted corrals and Annette planned for fabric curtains, new linens, cooking sup- plies, and the possibility of a baby. She added soft white batiste to her list and a bolt of white gauze fabric. She never learned to knit but put an instruc- tion book, needles, and yarn on her wants list.

"Why do you want yarn?" Cole asked.

"Scarves, mittens, and stocking hats would be nice next winter," she said, and he agreed.

Annette spent time in the barn when Cole worked on the corrals system, amazed at his ingenu- ity with projects.

"You know, you should try to get a patent on some of your projects. You've really got a streak of genius up there, Cole." She pointed to his thick crop of blonde hair.

He stopped his work and looked up. "What's a

patent?"

"I learned about them at school. You put your idea on paper with diagrams, measurements, and details and send the project information to the patent office in Washington, D.C. Once it's registered with the patent office, you own the idea. No one else can copy your idea or make your project unless they get permission from you and pay you for your patent or its use."

"I already have several plans drawn out in my plan book." He stopped and pulled a small book from a shelf. He tossed the notebook to her and resumed his work.

Annette spent an hour going through the book, amazed at his ideas and the intricate detail with which he explained and drew them out on paper. There were plans for a slotted corral and indoor plumbing that took dirty water outside the cabin. She saw a similar drawing for the same type of system under the kitchen basin, and a complete set of plans for a large stone house.

Original drawings for the pantry they used, marked 'complete' and a cold box in service near the creek marked 'rebuilt.' Annette marveled at how his mind must work, and then she remembered he all but taught himself to read and had read the Bible twice, a lengthy feat she felt sure she could never manage without direction.

She began to piece together the complex man she married who so willingly took care of her every need. She said a silent prayer thanking the Lord for him before she closed the notebook.

"I think I'll send for the patent papers for

your slotted corral to fill out in the spring when the pony express rider comes by if this is all right with you?"

"Sure, whatever you want to do is fine by me." He stopped and looked up again. "I suppose you saw the plumbing for the tub and the sink and want them both right away?"

"Yep," Annette said, and Cole laughed.

~ * ~

Ellie mounted the best horse in the barn and rode out into the clear winter sunlight. She wrapped up in a bear skin coat that had hung in the barn since she could remember. She needed to make the ride to Cole's and Annette's no matter what the weather.

Late February had found her completely out of food. Her hens stopped laying when she ran out of feed for them. They pecked at sparse vegetation and barely existed. She thought they would die, and she needed help. Her father, John, never returned. She ate all the beef gifted them at Christmas and there were no vegetables.

Her face and neck were slender, her stomach felt flat across the front of her torso and her hips had slimmed considerably. When she starred at her reflection in the glass of the window at night, she knew she looked thin. Her clothing hung on her frame, every dress too large, and she started taking in the seams, sharpening her sewing skills during the empty hours of the winter days.

She remembered the winter night when she thought she would die and thought she listened to her mother telling a story. Ellie decided she would

105

do what the girl in the story did and leave in the spring to find work sewing in a factory somewhere in the south. She would not go to Shreveport where she knew Bobby might be living with family.

The ride took longer than a couple of hours this morning, and finally she saw the cabin. By the time she arrived, Annette and Cole were on the porch. They watched her for a few minutes and noted she traveled at a slow pace. Cole stepped out, helped her down from the animal, and directed her inside with Annette.

"I'll take the horse to the barn and get him some feed and will back in few minutes." Cole looked at the emaciated animal and his heart sank. He could only try to give the animal some strength and relief, but he doubted the horse would make it another week.

Ellie sat quietly at the kitchen table and finally warmed enough to remove the bear coat. Annette deposited the coat on the wooden table near the fireplace to warm it.

The coffee finished perking and she poured a cup for Ellie. Ellie wrapped her fingers around the cup and drank slowly. She finally spoke when Annette placed a loaf of pumpkin bread on the table and began to slice the delicacy for her company.

"I haven't eaten in at least a week and I do not know where my father is. He left before Christmas."

Annette stopped and could not believe what she heard. She placed the bread on a plate and gave some to Ellie. Annette cautioned her to eat slowly so the bread would stay down, and Ellie complied.

Cole came in and joined the two women at the table and Ellie repeated her story.

"John left to take a few days' work and he said for me not to worry if he didn't come right back. He started leaving for weeks at a time after my mother died but he always returned with money and food. This time he hasn't come back. I'm starving and so are my animals."

Cole thought he might know how John came up with his money and the items he brought home but kept his thoughts to himself. Since the Wilks' arrived in the territory, everyone he knew came up missing food and stock and no one ever knew John to work a day in his life. Concerned about the length of John's absence, Cole thought he might have fallen prey to something or someone. He would begin searching the countryside looking for a body, or at least, clues to what might have happened.

"Please eat lunch with us and we'll figure out what to do for you, and how we can help," Annette said.

Annette finished preparing the side dish of mashed potatoes and asked Cole to pull the roast from the oven to cool for a few minutes and set it on the table. Annette stirred together the roux for gravy. They all enjoyed a large lunch and more coffee and dessert after the meal. By midafternoon, they all set out to load the buckboard with supplies and feed and take Ellie back home.

They left the cabin in early afternoon with a full load of horse feed, chicken feed, flour, corn-meal, beans, and salt pork in the bed of the buckboard wagon. Annette also parted with some of her

rationed coffee when she saw how much Ellie enjoyed the drink.

Ellie looked extremely thin and gaunt, and the
weight loss did not look good on her. She needed the
weight to balance out her large boned frame. Annette could tell Ellie lost most of the volume in her
hair and the once thick fringe of bangs hung limp
and flat against a pale white forehead.

"I'm going to board the horse in the barn. I
don't think the animal can make the journey back
yet. I'll bring him back in a couple of weeks after
the animal has gained some weight." Cole unloaded
the feed in the barn and then took the rest of the
supplies to the house before returning to the barn to
tend to the animals.

"Please sit down, Ellie, and regain your
strength. Tell me where you want the supplies
stored." Annette's heart ached for a neighbor who
could be near starvation death and she did not know
or help.

"The tall white wooden cupboard next to the
window is a good place," Ellie said.

Annette noted the cupboard was bare. She
stored away food items that would last at least two
or three months for Ellie alone, and a couple of
months if John came back.

Ellie sat silent the whole time Annette filled
the cupboards and then started preparations on the
stove for a pot of beans and salt pork.

"Does Cole love you?"

Annette stopped with her spoon mid-air and
turned to face Ellie. "He'll have to answer for himself, but I hope so, because I love him dearly and

108

wouldn't want to live a day without him."

Ellie seemed surprised at her answer. "Then you're not leaving in the spring when we travel to Mud Creek?" Ellie asked.

"Being here in the territory is not what I planned for my life, in fact, this is the opposite. Tony and I were going to live on a grand estate in California, and then everything changed. I feel like someone else took control and placed me where I needed to be." Annette paused for a moment to stir the pot on the stove.

"I left my home and set out to find a new and better life. I didn't know it would be with Cole. We read a passage in our Bible study last night that said, 'seek and ye shall find' or in another translation, 'you must seek to find,' and I believe because I left to seek a better life, Cole found me."

"Or maybe you found Cole."

Surprised at the depth of Ellie's words, Annette realized she found her fate with God's help and direction.

"I see what you're saying. My mother used to read the Bible aloud all the time," Ellie said, watching Annette cook. "I think you've changed Cole in a lot of ways. He's different."

They both heard Cole on the porch stomping the dirt from his boots before entering the cabin. Both girls laughed.

"Trained well, my dear." Ellie saluted Annette.

The beans cooked at a full, rolling boil while Annette made a batch of corn muffins and loaded them in the oven. "Take them out in exactly twenty minutes."

Ellie licked her lips and wrote down the time on a piece of paper. "Don't worry, I won't miss the time."

When Annette and Cole prepared to leave, Ellie gave her a firm hug. "Thank you. Thank you both for your help."

"I'll be back in a week with more feed. Feed all the animals twice a day until I get back. I don't know if some will make the week but keep the water buckets and feed bins full. The cow should start giving milk by then and the chickens laying eggs again."

They parted ways assured Ellie would survive until Cole and Annette returned in a week.

The ride home felt cold, and Annette nudged closer to Cole thinking about Ellie's questions. She decided to ask one more time, to put her mind at peace. "Were you going to marry Ellie before I came?"

"Not without a shotgun and a posse," Cole said, deadly serious. Annette's laughter rang out across the prairie west to the foot of the Rocky Mountains.

~Ten~
Mud Creek

$\mathcal{L}$ate March brought days of warm sunshine with cold nights. With only a few snows during the winter, the earth would take longer to turn green. Annette and Cole loaded into the covered wagon and set out for the prearranged meeting place to rendez-vous with Georgia and Tom Smith, and a new family who staked a claim west of the Smith homestead.

"Reverend Schmidt will make the ride with us from Ft. Atkinson where he serves as chaplain to the troops who stop for rest. Several more families you don't know yet will meet us along the way with their livestock and wagons. Most of them were there the day we married," Cole said.

"I'm sorry I don't think I can remember all their names," Annette confessed. She looked forward to the company and felt excited to make this trip.

When they pulled up to the Wilks' place, Ellie was ready to pull out in her buckboard with all her horses and milk cow. Her wagon was loaded with all the remaining food supplies Cole and Annette provided for her during the winter and she had stripped the cabin of blankets.

"She's got everything she owns loaded on the buck board and looks like she's planning to sell everything. All her clothes are probably in the small trunk under the buckboard seat," Cole noted.

"Ellie told me she would leave if her father

did not return by the spring trip."

Cole greeted Ellie. "So, you are going to sell out your stock and leave?"

"I can't go through another frigid winter," Ellie said.

Cole nodded and wondered if she would use the money for coach fare on the stage out of Mud Creek.

By the end of the first day, there were fifteen wagons, thirty riders on horses, about five hundred head of cattle, and fifty horses going to market. The first night the troop was jubilant with campfires, cooking, and people playing the fiddle and banjo. Cole introduced Annette to everyone and this time, she remembered their names.

Ellie sat quietly, but looked to be enjoying the company, and smiled at a joke or two. She cradled her coffee cup and ate from the potluck everyone brought to the campfire. Ellie brought some corn bread in a cotton bag, happy and proud to set out something to share.

Each day, the band set out at sunrise, eating cold leftover food from the night before. Cole prepared a small fire every morning for anyone who brought their pot of coffee for everyone to share.

Four more groups of riders, wagons, and cattle joined the group who made slow progress toward the cattle pens at Mud Creek. Cole handled the recount of cattle when the new groups joined, and the added task proved to be time consuming.

Each night, Annette asked Ellie to join them at either the Bible study or campfire and she began to meet with them regularly. Their friendship grew but she still felt Ellie held something back and would not give of herself. She laughed at the jokes and enjoyed the music but sat mute through the Bible lessons like a pouting child.

Annette knew Ellie seemed sad and marked her mood off to her father's disappearance. Cole rode out daily when they were still at the cabin, checking every place he could think of and did not find a trace of John. He feared the worst for him.

One evening Ellie opened up a little. "I'm traveling south where the weather is warm, maybe Louisiana or Georgia. I never want to be cold again. Aren't you from New Orleans? Is the climate warm down there?"

Annette's heart went out to her whenever they talked. "Yes, my mother is still there. We were cold when the rains came in the winter, but there's no snow like here." Annette stopped and took a deep breath. "I ran away from my mother, from my home."

Ellie's eyes flew open wide. "You mean you did what I'm going to do? You ran away? Why?"

Annette knew her sentence opened the floodgates and decided to tell Ellie her story. Everyone would find out eventually and sooner seemed better than later.

"My mother ran a brothel in downtown New Orleans. I never knew my father and I didn't want to be there anymore." She fell silent for a time, then added, "I think I might have been afraid I would turn out like my mother, so, I left."

"A brothel?" Ellie hesitated for a moment.

"You mean a house where men pay women..." Her voice trailed off and she could not even verbalize her thoughts.

"Yes. The oldest profession in the Bible. I did not want to repeat her life. I decided I would rather be dead than start down her path. When Tony came along and wanted to marry me, I ran away with him. I ran away from everything."

"Did you ever regret running away?"

"I should have been upfront with my mother and told her I was leaving whether she wanted me to or not. I feel like I betrayed her, but I didn't know how to get away."

"You could always write her a letter and tell her. Sometimes writing is easier than saying something to someone's face."

"Were you in love with Tony?"

Annette hesitated before answering. "I thought so. I thought I knew what love felt like, but I simply did not know relationships take time to grow and understand each other. I mistook attraction for love."

"What happened?"

"Tony was a handsome man but the longer I knew him, the uglier he got."

Both women exchanged looks of amusement and burst into laughter at the ridiculous sound of the sentence, knowing exactly what Annette meant.

"Some men are selfish and only think of themselves," Ellie said. "I knew a guy like that last summer before you came to our settlement. His name was Bobby Smith. He's Tom's younger brother. Georgia gave him room and board for the summer, so he could work, and then sent him packing to Kansas City in late August. He was good-looking too, but downright selfish, only thinking of himself. At first, I thought he might be the one for me. I soon realized he didn't care about me." She paused and sighed heavily.

"He said we would go to Kansas City and get married. Then we'd go to Shreveport where he knew he could find work. And one day, he rode out and never even said goodbye." Ellie looked at the ground for a long time and Annette knew the rest of her story would have to wait.

"I think you're right about writing a letter to my mother. I started writing her one, but never finished. Thank you, Ellie." Annette noted no response from Ellie, who appeared lost in other thoughts.

Annette was still sitting by the campfire with Ellie when Cole came by and sat down. "I have herding duty tonight and will be out with the cattle until early morning," he said.

"I think I'll work on my letter to my mother tonight," Annette said. "Good night Ellie." Ellie simply starred at the ground.

Cole walked Annette back to the wagon before meeting the men for herding duty. She began working on a new letter to her mother by the lamplight and decided to leave the letter at the post when they arrived in Mud Creek. This would be a long letter, so she took her time and started with the night she left with Tony.

The cattle drive took weeks and Annette used

Cole's almanac to track the days. Conversations with Ellie got longer, and Annette knew something haunted Ellie, and guessed Ellie's distress might have something to do with Bobby.

One evening after supper Ellie began to cry, confessing she deserved God's punishment for everything but would not give Annette details.

"You are already forgiven, even before you ask. Jesus died for your sins and mine. Simply ask Him to forgive you and you will start anew the next minute."

"No, God is punishing me."

"Sometimes we punish ourselves. God wants us to move on, to go forward. He doesn't want us to stop living and wallow in our past grief. He forgives us everything, so we need to forgive each other and ourselves, and start each day new. Place yourself in His hands and trust Him. He'll guide every decision you make, then you'll be in the right place." Annette asked Ellie to help her pray. The two of them sat huddled behind the wagon where no one could see and prayed together for forgiveness.

Cole saw the two women praying and smiled. During their childhood, he and Ellie both ran on the prairie barefoot, jumping over cactus without a second thought. They were fearless with only one incident frightening Ellie.

They came across the carcass of a newborn calf and recognized the small animal had been born with bad back legs. The carcass showed badly deformed rear leg bones. He remembered it was the only time he ever saw Ellie cry. His smile faded, and he knew something was wrong with Ellie. Her

116

damaged spirit needed a lift so she could run again. He hoped the prayers with Annette would help.

By the time the band of neighbors reached their destination, they all knew each other well. Annette collected a stack of recipes and shared some of her own. Ellie and Annette grew closer, but a cavern of space still existed between them.

~ * ~

Mud Creek bustled with groups of men talking. People, horses, and cattle walked the dirt streets. The small band pulled up outside the settlement near the pens and several people went to find the tents and log cabins used for saloons and stores.

Twilight turned to dark, and Cole stayed by the cattle with some of the other men, who kept the herd in a tight group for a final count the next morning.

Annette settled down into the blankets after she scrubbed herself head to toe from a bucket of water Cole brought her. She shampooed her hair and set out some clean clothing to wear in the morning.

She felt Cole come in sometime during the early morning hours and knew he must be tired from lack of sleep, but first light found him at the small campfire making coffee. She dressed in a hurry and went outside to sit with him. Cole brought the book with his bank balances and her letter to the patent office in Washington.

"There's a pony express post at the end of the street and we'll stop by first thing. Sometimes they have letters for the western territory on hold until a

117

rider is ready," he said.

They stopped by Ellie's buckboard and woke her. "We're going into town and will stop by the post first at the edge of town. I'll help you sell your horses if you want," Cole said.

Ellie bounded out of the wagon. "I also want to sell the wagon."

"Then you're leaving for sure?"

"Yes, I want to go south where the weather is warm, and I'm going to find work sewing, maybe in a factory or a shop."

Others from the troop walked with them and everyone stopped at the post first, a small wooden building with a large porch. There were two letters for Cole and he tucked them in his jacket pocket. They deposited the patent office request. There were no letters for Ellie and she looked disappointed.

They entered the cattle buyer's tent and got in the line. The line went outside and around the tent. Everyone appeared to be in good cheer when the price for cattle and horses moved to a new high. They left with vouchers until the final count at the livestock pens at the edge of the settlement.

The process took several hours and when Cole's and Annette's cattle were firmly in the pen, they went to the bank with their vouchers.

Ellie sold her horses and her one milk cow and went to find the livery stable, so she could sell her buckboard.

Cole and Annette entered the bank and sat in

the big chairs near the back until Timothy Hersey came out and greeted Cole with a firm handshake.

"Come in, come in. And who is this beauty you're parading around town?" he asked. His eyes never left Annette, and she blushed under his stare.

"This is my wife, Annette. We were married in the fall."

"Congratulations, my man, congratulations," he said sincerely.

Cole and Timothy had been friends since Timothy started a general store and boarding house at Mud Creek where the cattle pens originated. Cole understood his vision for a town and became one of his first new depositors in the bank.

They entered his private office and began Cole's business. Before the noon hour ended, Cole added Annette's name to all his accounts. They left the bank, found one of the nicer boarding houses in town with a dining room, and sat down for lunch. While they waited for their food, Cole went to the desk and rented them a large room with a bath.

When they were still eating, Ellie came in excited. "You won't believe the price I got for the buckboard."

"Please sit with us while we finish our meal," Cole said.

"Please take some money, I want to pay you back for the feed and supplies from the winter." Ellie held out some bills.

"No, there were enough supplies and sharing gave us pleasure. You'll need your money when you get to where ever you're going down south," Cole said.

"I'm thinking about Georgia or southern Louisiana, anywhere but Shreveport..." Ellie's voice trailed off, her face turned white and her lips went stone gray.

"What's wrong?" Annette asked.

Cole followed Ellie's stare and saw John in a fine suit with a red brocade vest and a gold pocket watch chain hanging from the vest pocket. John escorted a young woman on his arm and held a big cigar in his mouth. He talked and laughed with the young woman, not noticing the people at the table.

Cole pushed his chair back with a loud scraping sound on the wooden floor. "John Wilks?"

~Eleven~
The Crime

John turned and stared at Cole first, and then he saw Ellie. John's face turned bright red and he began to stutter. Ellie rose from her chair, glaring at her father, and ran from the room. Annette followed her, and they sat on the bench outside the boarding house close to the territory marshal's office.

Ellie began crying uncontrollably and Annette could not find words to console her. Soon the marshal came out to where the women were sitting. "You ladies need help?" He reached for Ellie's hand to comfort her and offered his clean, white handkerchief.

Marshal Tom Hale stood six feet tall, with a stocky build. His shoulders were broad, but his waist line tried to roll over his gun belt. His dark hair, flecked with a hint of gray at the temples, needed a good cut. A full mustache covered thin, grayish lips. He wore denim jeans and a dingy white shirt tucked into his jeans. With his gun belt tied down on his right leg, he walked with a swagger.

"This is Ellie Wilks. Her father, John, disappeared some months ago, and left her to starve. We all thought something bad happened to him and we were shocked to find him here in Mud Creek appearing to be a man of some wealth."

Ellie could not stop crying. The marshal placed his arm around Ellie and told her, "Don't you

121

worry little lady. I will take care of everything." He almost took possession of Ellie with his movements and Annette stepped back, repulsed by his authoritative actions. Cole came out of the boarding house and walked straight to the marshal's office to ask about John.

"John came to town right after the first of the year with a leather bag full of gold nuggets and cash. He said he found gold out west on his farm in a creek near his house. He said he came to Mud Creek to enjoy his newfound wealth. He stays at the boarding house and sees many different women from the saloon. He's been no trouble. He only gets drunk and spends money," the marshal said.

"There's no creek near John's house. The only creek is the one running on the back of my land. I've never seen any gold nuggets there. And John never kept cash in all the twenty years I've known him."

"He did have cash before he sold the nuggets. He bought fine clothing first, then pulled out a fancy gold pocket watch to hang on his vest. He sells a nugget every time he needs money. Goes through the cash pretty good."

He turned to Ellie. "Is this true? Did he leave you to starve?"

"Yes sir," Ellie answered. "I rode to Cole's and Annette's place and asked for food and they helped me. There is no creek on our land. Cole always gave us whatever water we needed."

"What about your mom or other children?"

"Ma died on my twelfth birthday and I have no siblings," Ellie said, eyes filled with tears. "He's gone off before lots of time for weeks, but never for this long. When he came back before, he always brought a little money and some food." Ellie sobbed, making it difficult for her to speak.

"I think we better get Mister Wilks to the office and ask some questions. Please, have a seat in my office, ma'am," he said to Ellie, treating her with the greatest respect. Ellie responded, aware of his attention and went inside his office.

"All of you, if you please." He motioned to Cole and Annette to take a seat and he left for the boarding house.

They waited for the marshal. Cole pulled out the two letters and looked again at the return addresses. One letter came from the sheriff in Kansas City and one from Edward William Fitzgerald also in Kansas City. Annette didn't say a word but watched Cole's face turn angry. She did not recall ever seeing him like this before, but he simply returned the unopened envelopes to his inside jacket pocket.

Marshal Tom Hale returned with John, minus the young lady, and took him directly to a chair at a large table. He motioned for his guests to join them on the opposite side of the table and he took out a long, white legal tablet of ruled paper.

Marshall Hale announced, "An official investigation is in progress and everyone present will answer all questions presented to them in a truthful manner, nothing more, nothing less, with no opinions thrown in, only the facts." He began with John. "Where did you obtain the leather pouch with gold nuggets and cash?"

"I found the nuggets in the creek on my land and the cash is mine. I've saved for a long time," he said nervously.

"Did you leave your daughter with enough supplies, feed for livestock, and food for herself before leaving?" Marshal Hale asked pointedly while writing down every word John Wilks said.

"I left like I always do, and she's always managed before. She worked a garden and there were chickens and a milk cow." John's defense sounded weak.

"Did you leave feed for the animals?"

"I guess there might have been some." John hung his head and did not look at Ellie.

"Ellie," marshall asked gently. "Tell me the truth, is there a creek on your land?"

"No, sir," Ellie said in defiance to her father. "The creek is on Cole's land and Cole let us have water whenever we needed."

"Were you aware your father saved cash somewhere?"

"No, sir. Whenever John got money, he found liquor first and bought food second," Ellie answered truthfully.

"Cole, to your knowledge is there a creek on John's land?"

"No sir. There's no creek."

"Did you come to Ellie's aide when she asked for help?"

"Yes sir. Annette and I supplied food for her and feed for the animals. Ellie and the animals were all starving. I'm ashamed I didn't realize sooner John never returned." Cole shook his head, looking at John.

"Ain't no crime to leave your kinfolk to fend

for themselves," John said.

"But stealing gold and cash is a crime." Marshall Hale leveled his gaze at John, and then turned to Cole. "Do you have any idea where John got gold nuggets and cash?"

"Yes sir, I do," Cole said with a firm voice, and Annette looked puzzled.

Marshal Hale took the bag from John Wilks and dropped the contents on the table with a loud clunk to display many gold nuggets, cash, and a pearl handled derringer with intricate scrolling across the handle.

Annette gasped when she saw an exact replica of Tony's derringer.

"One moment ma'am, your turn is next," Marshal Hale said, awaiting Cole's answer.

"I think John stole the leather bag from the body of Tony Dubois. John found Annette and Tony first and let the rest of us know a man died in a wagon and left a young woman alone who needed help. I think the bag stayed inside Tony's jacket, not in plain sight in the wagon, or Annette would have known."

"Only the facts Cole, not what you think. Do you have any evidence to support your assumption?"

"Yes, sir, I think I do." He pulled out the letters from inside his jacket pocket and deposited them on the table.

"I think I have seen a derringer like this one before. It looks like part of a set in Tony's items hidden in his wagon."

"Ma'am," marshal asked Annette, "Do you know anything about this?"

"I know Tony owned a derringer exactly like the one there on the table, but I didn't know he owned a pair. I also did not know he held gold nuggets or this much cash. I remember when he paid for the wagon and supplies in Kansas City, it took all the cash in his wallet. I never knew anything about a leather bag of gold nuggets." Annette took a deep breath.

"Just take your time ma'am, and continue to tell me what you know," the marshal said.

"Tony became ill and when we couldn't travel anymore, we stopped for a couple of days. John came to the wagon asking who we were and where we were going this late in the travel season. John asked me to step out of the wagon and he said he would check on Tony. He stayed in the wagon for a long time and when he came out, he said Tony stopped breathing from the high fever. I don't remember much after John said Tony was dead. I fell to the ground and cried."

"Tell me what you know, Cole, about Tony and the wagon."

Cole reached for the two unopened letters in front of him and handed them to Marshal Hale. "When I married Annette, and took her wagon to the barn, I found some items and a pearl handled derringer exactly like this one."

"The items were hidden in a compartment under a heavy trunk far too heavy for Annette to even move, much less lift. I did not tell Annette about the items right away because I thought she would leave if she found the means to do so. When I finally told her, I believe she knew nothing of their existence."

"Annette related an incident to me about Tony and said we should write the sheriff in Kansas City, and we did. We told him everything we'd found and asked who the owners of the items might be. Here are the two letters I got this morning at the post. One is from the sheriff in Kansas City, and the other is from Edward William Fitzgerald. EWF matches the initials on some of the jewelry I found in the wagon. I'll let Annette tell you about the incident in Kansas City."

Everyone turned to Annette when she began relating the incident about the night Tony ran back to the wagon in Kansas City. "He told me he played cards and some of the sore losers started chasing him, but he managed to outrun them."

"Did you know where he went to play cards?"

"No, sir. But I did smell gunpowder on him when he came back to the wagon. I knew to be afraid of him by then, and I was too frightened to ask him if he'd fired his gun, but I knew the answer from the smell."

"Why were you afraid of him?"

"Because he'd struck me before and I knew his moods by then. I needed to go to my side of the wagon and be quiet."

Cole looked shocked. His heart ached for her when he reached out to touch her face. "I'm sorry I never asked you about his treatment of you before." Cole apologized and wiped away the tears streaming down her face.

"Cole, may I have your permission to open and read the two letters in the envelopes?"

"Of course. They confirm our story."

127

Annette nodded her consent, and the marshal read in silence. When finished, he replaced each of the letters back into their respective envelopes.

Marshal Hale then stood and handcuffed John. "John Wilks, you are hereby under arrest for the theft of items from the body of Tony Dubois."

John did not speak when the marshal placed him in a cell, then returned to the table to finish his questions.

"Who prepared Tony's body for burial?" Marshal Hale asked Cole.

"Several of us men and the preacher, but John did not help us."

Then Marshal Hale turned to Annette and asked, "Ma'am did you ever see the body of Tony Dubois after you were told he died?"

"No sir. I only saw his body wrapped in a blanket ready for burial." Annette frowned.

"Cole, take these ladies back to the boarding house and gather all men who helped ready Tony's body for burial and bring them back here, please," Marshal Hale said. "The ladies will not be needed for this discussion."

Cole sat motionless for a moment. "Ladies, we will find you a table and some hot tea at the restaurant in the boarding house while we finish this business."

He escorted both ladies to the dining area and picked a table in the corner near the window, so they could have a full view of Main Street and the marshal's office. He directed staff to provide anything they might need, starting with hot tea. Cole left his signature on the bill at the counter before

looking for the neighbors who helped bury the body
of Tony Dubois.

~Twelve~
Finding the Truth

Marshal Tom Hale convened the next part of the investigation with the heavy door to the cell area securely closed. He introduced himself to the men present and brought the group up to date on the investigation thus far. "I've arrested John Wilks for the theft of gold nuggets, cash, and a pearl handled derringer from the body of Tony Dubois."

"If you are the men who prepared the body for burial, I have some questions for you." He cleared his throat. "Reverend Schmidt, did you see any marks on the body of Tony Dubois when you assisted in preparation of his body for burial?"

"No marks, but I did think a healthy young man—" Reverend Schmidt started to tell his story and the marshal stopped him.

"Only the facts, sir. Were there any marks on the neck of the victim?"

"No marks on the neck," Reverend Schmidt said.

"How did the dead man's face appear? Eyes open or closed? Mouth open or closed?"

"His mouth was wide open like he was trying to scream, and his eyes were wide open too, kind of bugged-out almost. Scariest thing I ever seen."

"Were there red marks in the whites of his eyes?"

"Yes, like he'd been drinking. Both eyes were bloodshot as I have ever seen."

Marshal Hale looked at all the men. "Is Reverend Schmidt's description accurate as to how you would describe the dead man's face?"

They all nodded in agreement.

"Did anyone of you see other marks on the man named Tony Dubois?"

"No marks," Reverend Schmidt said, and they all nodded in agreement.

"Only a terrified look on his face. And we could not get his eyes to close or his jaw to snap shut. The jaw locked in place, so we covered his head with a second blanket. We did not want the women folk to see the body, and certainly not Annette," Cole said.

"I'm afraid we have a murder investigation," Marshal Hale said. "You see, when someone is suffocated with a pillow or strangled, he opens his mouth attempting to breathe before death locks the jaw. His eyes are wide open and the strain of the lungs struggling for air often causes hemorrhages in the whites of the eyes. A man dying of a high fever usually goes to sleep or into convulsions, but the whites of the eyes do not have read streaks, and a convulsion clamps the jaw shut. I believe Tony Dubois was suffocated."

Cole put his head in his hands and wondered at his wife being in the hands of thieves, murderers, and wife beaters. He wept at his own lack of care for her the first day when he confronted her at the grave. He cried for the way he treated her those first weeks, demanding work from her until she dropped onto her tiny cot exhausted.

He treated her like a hired servant with no concern for her feelings. He did not treat her with the care and dignity she deserved. He did not show her compassion in a horror-stricken time and marveled at her strength in pulling through without lashing out at anyone. He sat for a long while before he could rise from the chair.

The men agreed they would not repeat the horrible condition of the dead man's face until the testimony became necessary at the upcoming trial.

The group discussed how to care for the animals back home another two weeks while they waited for the trial. Each family had laid out feed for hired hands to distribute to their livestock before they left but no one prepared for an extra few weeks of absence.

The group decided to send two men who were not involved in the burial of Tony Dubois, back to the homesteads to aid in the care of the animals still at home. Those animals were the start of the next herd and extremely important.

Marshal Hale stood on the front porch of his office at the jail. He leaned against the post and took out some tobacco and paper and rolled a cigaretter. He thought for a long while and then dispatched a rider for the territory judge before dark.

Cole walked back to the boarding house with several of the men from the cattle drive. Marshal Hale went with them. Annette and Ellie sat at the dining table. Cole cleared his throat and announced, "Marshal Hale has charged John Wilks with the murder of Tony Dubois."

Annette sat stunned for a long time. "What happened?"

Ellie sat deathly silent and pale white.

"The investigation revealed Tony might not have died of a high fever but instead," Cole hesitated, "he might have been suffocated. The details will come out in the trial. So, we will be here for a couple of weeks at least, waiting for the judge to get here and hold trial. I've asked the boarding house manager if we can keep our rooms, and Ellie too. We do not need to stay in the wagon through all this. We need the comfort of a roof over our heads."

"I'll go with you and take care of Ellie's expenses. She's been through enough and you've helped out far beyond what a neighbor should have to do," Marshal Hale said, never taking his eyes from Ellie when he spoke. The two men left the women and went to the boarding house desk.

~ * ~

Annette looked out the windows of the dining room and quietly drank her coffee. She suddenly remembered Magnolia and her mother and longed to tell them everything. She would keep adding to the letter she worked on every day and wondered if she would ever see them again. Tears well up in her eyes.

"I miss my mother and Magnolia. I'm writing a letter to them." Annette looked at Cole and smiled. "I want to tell them about everything and let them know you are taking care of me."

"We've got a couple of weeks at least before

the trial. Is there anything special you'd like to do?"

"I need to replenish my fabric and thread and of course, get the list of supplies filled."

"We can work on the list anytime you're ready." Cole turned and saw Ellie come down the stairs.

Annette followed Cole's gaze and wondered what Ellie would do. Her hair swept up on the sides, hung in long loose curls down her back. Her fringe of thick glossy bangs shone this morning when she approached the marshal's table and asked him a question. He motioned for her to sit down but Annette could not hear the conversation. The marshal seemed captivated with Ellie and leaned in to talk to her.

Annette noticed Ellie wore the same dress since they arrived and made a note to ask the inn keeper at the boarding house about laundry services.

After a morning of coffee and a country breakfast, everyone went to the front desk at the same time. Cole signed the breakfast bill and asked to speak to the marshal at his office.

The marshal turned to Ellie and asked, "Could you wait a bit before coming over to talk to your father?"

"Yes, I can wait a bit," she said and went with Annette to arrange for laundry services.

The two men made their way to the marshal's office.

"I deposited the jewels and the first derringer in a safe deposit box at the bank when I first came into town. I removed the items from the eaves of the barn and packed them back into the bottom of the covered wagon before I left our homestead. My intention was to deposit the items in a locked vault in the bank with ownership to be determined by law enforcement and judicial offices," Cole said and handed over the key to the safety deposit box.

"If you will go with me to the bank, we can put your name on the box. I never dreamed there could be a murder involved. How did you know?"

"I've seen crime enough to know what happened. Thieves steal from thieves." Marshal Hale placed the key to the bank box in his vest. "Gold makes a bad man evil and then he always takes the next step. He's gotten away with illegal activity for so long, he gets careless, and he keeps taking the next step."

Both men agreed the solid bank vault should hold all items and letters of instruction and to release to the marshal what would be necessary for the trial. Cole added a detailed listing of all contents to the letters and placed them with the post to mail to the owner. Cole and Annette's signatures were on statements releasing the second leather bag and contents to the rightful owner.

Cole saw Ellie and Annette returning to the boarding house after securing laundry services. He caught up with them. "I need to talk with Ellie."

"Of course," Annette said and went back to the boarding house.

"Ellie, are you on your way to the jail? I'd like to speak wth you first."

They sat on a bench on the shady side of the building. "How are you making your way through all of this?"

Ellie could not answer and began to weep. She felt shame over her father actions and was filled with her own thoughts of self-pity and sadness even before the events here in Mud Creek. She walked with her head down and expected the worst from everybody and everything.

"Ellie," Cole said firmly and put both hands on her shoulders. "You have to be strong. I see something in you giving up. You seem to be looking for a way out, and there is no way out of pain and misery except what way you make. The world does not owe you anything, Ellie. Nobody can fix things for you except you."

"I can't. I can't keep going every day."

"You have to move forward. Don't let the wolves pull you down."

Ellie stopped crying and looked at Cole in horror. She opened her mouth to speak but nothing came out, and Cole suspected she thought of the calf carcass abandoned on the prairie so many years ago, when they were children.

"There is nothing wrong with your legs. You are strong, you can run, you can work. I saw you fall from the barn one day and get up and walk back to the house. A few days later, you were outside playing again. I remember being happy you were back outside. Your life is a lot different since we were kids. But you cannot change what your father did, only how you react to his actions. You can get up from anything, Ellie. You are a fine, strong woman." He moved his hands from her shoulders and prayed she heard his words with her ears and her heart.

"His actions only determine your life if you let them. Give up being down about your predicament and change your actions. Only you can change whatever is bothering you. Pray for help to heal your heart. God will give you strength and healing."

Ellie stopped crying, wiped her eyes, and took a deep breath. "Thank you, Cole. I am not going down," she said with determination. Ellie stood and went to the jail to face her father.

Marshal Hale opened the door to the cell. "John, your daughter will be here soon, so get out of your bunk and wash your face and hands and straighten your clothing." The deputy gave him a washbasin and a towel but no razor.

"Please, can I have my belt so my pants won't fall around my ankles?" John asked.

Marshal Hale ordered his deputy to provide him with his belt for the visit only and not to take his eyes from his prisoner for a single minute for all the time he wore the belt.

Cole found Annette waiting outside the boarding house when they heard a scream from the jail. They both ran to the marshal's office along with several other of the town's people. When they reached the door, they could see John's feet dangling in the cell and the deputy unconscious on the floor outside the cell.

Marshal Hale grabbed his keys, unlocked the door, and took John Wilks body down from the belt loop. The marshal's attention then turned to his deputy's nasty gash to the head.

Ellie collapsed in a heap on the floor in front

of her father's cell.

"I never lost a prisoner before," Marshal Hale said in shock.

Annette applied pressure to the deputy's wound until he regained consciousness and began answering Marshal Hale's questions.

"He acted like he choked on something and when I got to the cell he reached through the bars and pulled my head hard against the metal bars. Don't remember anything after he pulled me against the bars." The deputy looked down, he knew the marshal did not like what he told him.

"Cole, would you go to the boarding house and bring the doctor here?" Marshal Hale asked, and Cole bolted out the jail door.

Marshal Hale turned to Ellie, scooped her up in his arms, and carried her to a cot at the end of the cells. He laid her down gently and began speaking to her, but Annette could not hear the conversation.

Cole brought the doctor back to the jail and they watched him examine the deputy. "I think he needs some stitches and someone to watch him, so he doesn't go to sleep for a few hours."

The doctor pronounced the prisoner deceased by hanging and looked to where Ellie sat in shock. "Cole, will you help bring the deputy back to my office, so I can sew the nasty gash on his head?"

After Cole and the deputy left, the doctor went to Ellie. "You're to come by my office in an hour, I want to talk to you."

Annette wanted to comfort Ellie, but the marshal had her attention for the time being, so she walked back to the boarding house behind the deputy, Cole, and the doctor. Annette parted company with them at the boarding house stairs and went up to her room. She needed some space, just a little quiet, and ordered coffee. She knew tea would not be enough today.

When Cole returned to their room, she asked, "Do you know why the doctor wanted to see Ellie?"

"He said she looked deathly pale, and he's concerned about the dark circles under her eyes." Cole poured a cup of coffee and starred at the black liquid in his cup.

~ * ~

Only a few people attended the funeral with most of the group who traveled to Mud Creek choosing not to attend, but every family sent at least one representative.

The cemetery perched atop a hill at the edge of town and surrounded by trees felt secluded, and the new spring crop of grasses and wildflowers peeked through the soil. Annette was silent, remembering the last funeral she attended months earlier. Tears finally flowed for Tony when she realized he died at the hands of a murderer who only wanted his money and gold for personal pleasure.

How could selfishness get so far out of control in someone's soul they would steal and murder to get what they wanted? Did Tony shoot someone when he took the money, gold, and jewelry in Kansas City?

She knew the gut feelings of fear she had experienced back then were on target. She would never ignore those feelings and instincts again.

139

Ellie stood motionless when they laid her father into the ground and Marshal Hale swept her away before the dirt fell on the pine coffin.

"She's been spending a lot of time with the marshal. They eat together, and he barely lets her out of his sight. Maybe he is her clean start," Annette said.

"I hope so," Cole said.

~ * ~

Behind the closed doors of the marshal's office, Tom Hale surveyed Ellie from head to toe. He handed her two of the gold nuggets. "You take these nuggets and they'll help you get to where you're going to make a clean start." Marshal Hale closed her fist around the shiny, gold rocks.

Ellie starred at Marshal Hale. All this time, she thought he was above reproach and completely honest and good. She was speechless when he fell from the high pedestal upon which she placed him.

Marshal Hale is a thief, a common thief like my father, taking other's property for his own use.

She would not accept the nuggets and tried to put them back in his hands. He encircled her with strong arms and pressed her close to his chest. Then he moved in for a kiss and Ellie struggled to free herself.

"Leave me alone, let me go," she cried, and tried to step away, but he held tight.

"Why you ungrateful little slut," he said under his breath. "After all that I've done for you!" He seemed truly shocked at her reaction to his advances.

"I know you have kept company with men before. Doc said you suffered a miscarriage. What's the matter, am I not good enough?"

"I don't want the nuggets and I don't want your attentions," Ellie said firmly. She turned her face from him and he finally released her from his iron grasp. She dropped the nuggets on the table and bolted out the office door, for the safety of the boarding house.

Ellie knew from the posted schedule that the stage would be pulling in the next morning. She planned to catch the stage to Kansas City, then make her journey south or anywhere but here in Mud Creek. She locked her boarding room door securely behind her and wedged a wooden chair under the black metal and glass knob and began packing.

~ * ~

Annette and Cole greeted the spring morning with enthusiasm. Cole checked them out of the boarding house and secured their horses from the livery. The supplies were ready at the general store to be loaded into their wagon. Cole added a surprise for Annette, one of the new Singer treadle sewing machines hidden under a tarp in the freight wagon. He saw her examining the machine at the general store and pretended not to notice.

They saw Ellie come out of the boarding house with her small duffel bag in hand. Ellie walked directly to the stage office and went in. Cole and Annette looked at each other and decided to wait until she came out. Annette wanted to say goodbye and make sure Ellie knew she cared about her and find out what she would do. The stage pulled up in front of the stage office and Ellie came out, ready to load but stopped when she saw Annette and Cole and waved at them to come to the stage.

"I'm leaving for Kansas City in a few minutes. Then I am heading somewhere warm and I am going to make a new life for myself. I've decided on Georgia." Ellie smiled broadly and gave them each a hug.

"Let me load your bag on top." Cole grabbed her bag and climbed up the coach.

"How strange, I'm the one who wanted to leave in the spring and get a coach to anywhere, and now we're trading places and you're going," Annette said.

Ellie laughed, a sound Annette had only heard a few times, and said, "I thought I wanted to marry Cole, and now you are married to him."

Ellie took Annette's hand and squeezed. "I'm off to find my own Cole and he's not here in Mud Creek, for sure. Thank you, Annette, for telling me I am new in God's eyes and today is the day I can go forward with a clean start." She gave Annette another hug. "Thank you too, Cole," she said looking up to where Cole crouched on top of the coach with the bags.

Cole tucked Ellie's bag safely into the pile atop the coach and cinched the rope securely over the pile. He stepped down to the wheel in a single stride and hopped to the ground. The driver mounted the seat and took the reins.

"All aboard," the driver called out.

"Good luck, Ellie," Cole said. "Please write us and let me know what you want done with your land.

I can help you sell if you want."

"I didn't think about the homestead," Ellie replied then pondered for a moment. Even though she now owned the land, she knew she did not want to live there anymore. "I'll write and let you know." Cole helped her up the step, and she waved from the coach window as the driver pulled out.

"I'm worried, Cole. We should have given her some money, so she can at least eat. What will she do?"

"She'll eat. I pinned a roll of cash inside her duffle bag. The funds will be enough to get her started until she gets a paycheck."

Annette squeezed his hand. "Always taking care of others."

~ * ~

Ellie sold her place to the doctor who came from Mud Creek, and asked Cole to take care of the transfer of the money and the deed. The doctor started building a large cabin on the Wilks' place. His wife, JoAnn, came out with him to start a schoolhouse like the one at Mud Creek. He also planned to go forward with the planting of a cotton crop when several large bags of cotton seed were delivered. The doctor wired money to Ellie to pay for her father's expense of freight and seed.

~ * ~

Annette sat on a bale of hay in the warm summer sunshine coming in the south end of the barn. She petted the new kittens nestled in her lap. They slept on the crisp fabric of her new apron as she opened mail delivered by the Pony Express rider.

Annette opened the patent office paperwork

143

and studied the forms for Cole's patents. She knew he would have at least one by the end of the year.

She opened the letter from Edward William Fitzgerald and read. *"Tony shot me in the leg and I now suffer a continuous limp from the wound but will soon have a new surgery in London to correct the limp. Before I leave for England, I wanted you to know I deposited five thousand dollars in reward money in your name at the Mud Creek bank.*

I am grateful beyond words for someone who would care for my items and try to find the rightful owner to return them. The jewelry has belonged in my grandmother's collection passed down through the generations and we continued to use the initials EWF when naming offspring. It is with grateful thanks for your kind Christian heart that I express my desire to meet you one day and shake your hand."

Annette thought about the hefty sum of money. The funds were small in comparison to other funds Cole accumulated but an idea struck her. Their small settlement needed a general store and the sum might make a store possible. She would have to tell Cole about her idea and see if he thought it might be workable.

Annette felt the baby kick inside of her and the kittens turned to stare at the growing bump at Annette's mid-section. They jumped down and she stood to rub her back. She went to check the mare in the stall on the other side of the barn. The spirited horse would be dropping a colt any day. *By Christmas we can both jump again.* She patted the mare's nose, then folded the letters and walked out

144

of the barn into the warm sunshine.

Annette saw Cole coming from the pasture behind the cabin where he directed stonecutters and artisans on the construction of their home. He also supervised laborers who were turning soil for a large garden area and an apple orchard. She smiled broadly when he came into sight. *I guess I got more than I bargained for, so much more.*

~The End~

145

Made in the USA
Columbia, SC
27 September 2018